The Last Visitor

Dedication

This book is dedicated first and foremost to my Father in Heaven, Yah, who by His grace and mercy through faith in His Son, Yahoshua, my mediator, saved me, called me, and sanctified me through the prompting and convicting of His Holy Spirit. Without Yah, I am nothing.

I also dedicate this book to my family: my precious daughter, Tracee, who is my best friend and helps me in so many different ways. Without her, this book would not have been possible; my mother, Mable who gave me life; my stepfather, Otis who raised me; my brother, Donald, my sister, my niece, Britney; my son Kirk and his family; my grandchildren: Allaria, Michal, and Lanie; my many aunts, uncles, cousins, and friends.

This book is a legacy to my relatives who once lived in Coolidge—people unknown to many, people whose visits here on earth were brief, yet whose presence had a profound and life-changing impact upon my very existence. I cannot, and will not, ever forget them: Big Mama, Clarence White, Sr., Mary Emma White, James White, Viola White, Grandma Juniel, Miss Sarah, Ivory Joe, Nellie White, Rayfield White, Sydney White, Roxie White, Charles White, Rose Sampson, Haywood Sharp, Lee Arthur White, Ricky Gamble, Earl Sampson, and especially my buddy and pal, Michael Sampson, who I still miss dearly.

The Last Visitor

Elizabeth Abigail James

FM Publishing Company

THE LAST VISITOR

Published by
FM Publishing Company
P.O. Box 10744
Casa Grande, AZ 85130-0108
United States of America
www.fasthelpministries.com

1993

LOS ANGELES

Chapter One

Smoke. Luther's long pointy nose detected it as soon as he stepped off the bus. Not cigarette smoke—more like trash burning and crackling inside those big, rusty barrels just outside of Coolidge.

Tension. Luther could feel it. As thick as the Los Angeles smog that slapped him in the face. He didn't know which was worse: the smoke, the smog, or the people pushing and shoving as they hustled and bustled, trying to claim their bags. He could hear screams, and cars honking and screeching in the distance. He could just make out the tale-end of obscenities flying back and forth.

It reminded him of how upset some of the men in Coolidge were two years ago when the Minnesota Twins pulled an upset over the Atlanta Braves 4-3 in the World Series. Luther understood that anger. But here, people seemed angry just because they had to get out of bed in the morning.

His son had described Los Angeles countless times, and Luther had been in bus stations before, but tonight he felt strangely uncomfortable. This was nothing like he'd seen before. The night air was too cold for summertime. Not at all like the "Sunny California" his son talked about. So far, Luther decided, he wasn't having a good time. Even the bus driver had accused him of smoking in the bathroom on the bus. He had felt embarrassed and humiliated, being called to the front of the bus, falsely accused, and then called a liar when he said he didn't smoke. But he had managed to regain his composure amid all the stares and giggles.

Luther was determined that his visit not be ruined. No, this visit would be special. The bus driver was in a deep discussion with another driver. Luther ambled over to him.

"Excuse me, can you tell me where I might find a phone?"

"Inside, old man. Inside." There was irritation in the driver's voice.

Luther picked up his suitcase. It was light. He was only staying in Los Angeles a few days. As he pushed through the doors to the station, his nose and right eye twitched in unison. His nose, from the reek of pine cleaner failing to cover the smell of stale cigarettes, sweat, beer and urine. His right eye twitching like that always whenever trouble was about to happen.

He reached in his jacket pocket and pulled out the letter from his son Jake. He had to get to a phone. Jake would be expecting his call. It wasn't every day that a man's son graduates from UCLA Law School—with honors. Luther smiled. What do doctors know? Cancer. Four years ago they told him he'd never see this day. Sure, he'd been down a few times, but not out for the count. It had taken everything he had to fight for this day. Fifteen pills a day. But his son was more than worth it.

Luther's right eye still twitched, but he smiled bravely at the stony black faces that almost sneered at him as he wobbled over to the pay phones. "Hello," he said, with a polite wave. No response.

People were huddled together. There were loud whispers, spitting out words in disgust. Luther caught a few words here and there.

". . . it was bound to happen . . ."

"What'd they expect, anyhow?"

". . . white folks, hmph!"

". . . honkys always the same—just plain tired—tired, I tell you!"

Luther set his bag on the blue wire bench near the baggage lockers. He saw the phones against the wall. He was fascinated by the electronic message board displaying bus arrival and departure schedules. Coolidge could definitely use one of those. No, most of the folks were too stingy. Would probably vote it down.

He almost ran into a black woman with a sleeping baby draped across her shoulder. "Sorry, ma'am. I didn't see nobody there."

She stopped chewing her gum and glared at him. Her nostrils flared as she put the phone to her chest. "And what do I look like, white man?" she said, shaking her head.

Luther excused himself and found an empty phone away from the woman, who rolled her eyes, and then resumed her gum chewing and conversation. Luther picked up the receiver, then remembered he had no coins for the call. He noticed a coin machine next to the vending machines. As he took a dollar out of his wallet, he found himself with company. Luther's nose was aware of the woman even before his eyes were.

"Excuse me, sir, can you spare some change so I can get a sandwich?"

She had a Spanish dialect. Short, dirty blonde hair stuck out from all sides of her beige knitted cap. She tugged on a white rust-stained sweater that hung down over grease-stained, lime-green polyester pants. The pants were just shy of hiding a pair of pale yellow socks, protruding through faded blue tennis shoes.

"Well, lemme see," Luther said. "How much you think you need for a sandwich?"

The woman smiled, exposing missing and half-rotten teeth. "How much you got to spare?"

"Well, I might get hungry too. We could split a sandwich, if that's okay?"

The woman moved closer. The smell of liquor grew stronger. She turned up her nose and her voice got louder. "You mean to tell me, you can't spare a measly little bit of change to help a poor old woman in need?"

Luther glanced around at the angry faces staring at him. Quickly, he handed her two dollars. The woman grinned triumphantly.

"Thank you kindly," she said, stuffing them into her bra. "Now that's a real kind man."

Luther sighed as the woman walked over to a man standing at another vending machine. A sharp pain rumbled through his backside. He looked at his watch. Quarter to nine. Time to take his medicine. He moved slowly back to the bench where he'd left his bag. It was gone. Luther panicked, looking around him. There was a tap on the window outside of the bus station. Five black teenagers. One of them, the bigger of the five, was grinning and holding up his bag. Luther reckoned that fifty years ago, that teenager and Hawk—that's me, I'm Hawk—could have been twins. Luther, now clutching his side in agony, pushed his body through the doors. It was hard to talk.

"I believe that's my bag."

They laughed. "Oh really, old man," the bigger of the five said. "I found it. What proof you got it's yours?"

"Please, I left it on the seat inside. It is mine," Luther insisted.

The boy grinned. "Well, maybe it is yours. What you thinking of doing about it?

Luther grimaced. The pain was getting stronger. "Please, I just want my bag back." He looked back inside the station. The people who'd been watching turned their backs. "I don't want no trouble." His eye kept twitching.

The biggest one smacked his smoke-stained lips and winked at his partners. "What you say, fellas. It's five of us and one of him."

One of the others twisted his baseball hat forward again on his small head. "Seems that's the way it's supposed to be."

"Yeah," said the others, nodding in agreement.

The biggest one smiled again. "Yeah—that's right—"

They made a move towards Luther who put up his hands in defense. "Please, I'm sick. I need my medicine!"

The biggest one pointed to the bag as he held it in mid-air. His words seem to laugh as he spoke. "Oh, in here. Well, let's just see."

He tore open the bag, and Luther watched helplessly as they threw out his shoes, slacks, shirt, underclothes, toiletries and his bottles of pills. The boy stopped.

"Now what's this?" The boy dropped the bag and took out a small neatly wrapped package. He ripped it open and admired the baseball covered with signatures of famous ball players.

No, Luther thought, they can't have that. He let go of his side long enough to lunge forward and snatch the ball. Then he ran with it as fast as his age-old legs could carry him towards the end of the station. Not looking down, he tripped over some beer bottles and his chin slammed into the cement. His ears rang and his head went numb.

The biggest boy's nostrils glared when they caught up with him. "Nobody, but nobody takes nothing away from me!" He kicked Luther in the side.

Luther tried to cry out but no sound would emerge. Tears rolled down his red cheeks. The teenager picked up one of the beer bottles and the others followed suit. Crack! The bottles broke over Luther's head. They hit him repeatedly. He didn't bother to count the number of times the glass cut into his body, but he pulled the ball into his chest and never let go of it. His hands, face, head and clothes were soaked in blood.

"You white honky! This is for Rodney King!" was the last thing he heard before he faded out.

The people inside the station had witnessed the crime. They had sensed it coming. Secretly, they'd probably hoped it would come. Vicariously, they shared in delivering the hate-filled blows to the old man outside. Make the white man pay. Justice must prevail. Luther was no longer a person with flesh and blood. He had become their whipping post. Hadn't they suffered four hundred years of slavery? Torn from their mothers' bosoms. Sold, raped, beaten, hanged, whipped, lied to and repeatedly humiliated. They'd come a long way, but the road was too long. This was 1993.

Two years ago, what to them was unthinkable had happened: five white policeman were acquitted for brutally and candidly beating a black man named Rodney King. Fifty-four blows to the body and head. All videotaped. But they reckoned the jurors had looked the other way. The people's anger burned within. So let the city burn, they cried. A year later they rioted. They looted. They destroyed. But they were still angry. So, let this old white man die. They'll look the other way, too. Just like the jurors did. Why should they care anymore?

But somebody did care. The ambulance came. Luther was unconscious, but still breathing. The ambulance screamed down the street towards the hospital through the smoke-filled air. Those remaining in the station did not feel justified. They did not feel vindicated. They felt ashamed. They still felt beaten.

The ambulance pulled up to the emergency room. The paramedics quickly transported Luther's stretcher through the doors. The doctor who had received the call met them at the door.

"Prepare him for OR, stat!"

The ambulance driver handed Luther's jacket and bag to the registration nurse as the others rolled him into the operating room.

The nurse sighed, reaching out for the bag. "What do we have here?"

The driver spoke without looking up from the form he was filling out. "Male. Caucasian. Mid-sixties, maybe. Severe cranial and body lacerations. Unconscious. Pretty bad shape." He stopped writing and looked up. "Better notify his next of kin." The driver turned to leave and then remembered. "Oh, this is his also," he said, handing the bag with the blood-stained baseball to the nurse.

She shook her head. "Over a baseball?" She searched through Luther's jacket and found his wallet. She took out the driver's license and stared in shock at the oh-so-familiar smiling face of her friend Luther. Luther Bernard Rawlings, the license said. Born

February 12, 1923. 6' 2", 220 pounds, 57 James Street, Coolidge, Arizona. She clutched at her chest and felt dizzy.

"Olivia, are you all right? another nurse called to her.

"What? Oh, yes—I'm all right." Olivia picked up the phone and called me.

I almost dropped the phone and my heart skipped a beat. I felt the life ooze out of me. "Are you sure it's Luther?"

"Yes, Hawk—I'm sure."

"Don't worry. Me and Tommy Lee'll track down young Jake and let him know."

Luther had fought for what was rightfully his at the bus station. Now he was fighting for his life as the doctors operated. The black teenagers probably felt they were fighting for Rodney King and the dignity that was rightfully theirs. Rodney and those boys had their battles, and Luther had his. Unfortunately, Luther Rawlings didn't know Rodney King. Those boys didn't know Luther. How could they? They never bothered to find out. Anybody in Coolidge would have told them, had they taken the time to listen. But nobody alive knew Luther better than me—Hawk—two years older than Luther. Do you have the time to listen to his story?

LUTHER'S STORY

ARIZONA

Chapter Two

My name is Hawk. Hawk Williams, if you want it all. I've known Luther for more years than I care to remember. Of course, he was white and I was black. Not that it made any difference. Not in the end. We were friends. Good friends. We must've shared at least a hundred-and-one stories back and forth. I guess I've heard every one of Luther's stories and shared his innermost thoughts, because after a while he started repeating himself. It didn't matter, though. Luther would get so excited about telling you something, that even if you heard it before, he made it sound fresh and new.

As far as I know, Luther had never been out of Arizona before he got beat up. He was born in Florence Hospital, because there wasn't one in Coolidge. His mama was one of the lucky ones. We used to call Florence the "Killing Hospital." Most folks who went in never came out alive. Of course "most folks" meant "black folks."

The first time Luther had ever been to Phoenix was when somebody gave him two free tickets to the Cardinals' game. Luther fell in love with baseball when he was five years old. Babe Ruth had just joined the Yankees. Luther was so proud of being a "south-paw" just like The Babe. It looked funny to me, though, the way Luther wrote—like he had the paper upside down. Years later, when they retired The Babe's Number 3, Luther said it would always be his favorite number.

Luther never liked Scottsdale. He said the place gave him an eerie feeling. His mama used to clean houses up that way. Luther said folks always expected him to know the difference between a salad fork and a dinner fork. As if it really made a difference which was which. The only place Luther swore he'd never visit was Prescott. That's where he heard his daddy was supposed to be living. Luther never called him "my daddy." He always said, "that man."

You could always tell when you were coming into Coolidge. There was Shopes Market if you were coming in from the south, and the Dairy Queen if you were coming in from the north. Folks would always give those two landmarks as a starting place whenever they had to tell a visitor how to get somewhere in or out of town.

Luther and his mama had it pretty rough during the Great Depression. Seems like everybody had it rough during that time. Coolidge and the towns around it were mostly farm towns. Picking cotton wasn't a disgusting, degrading thing like it is today. You got four cents a bushel and were glad for it. Silly as it seemed, the rich folks were having a harder time than we were. Stock market crashed, and folks were crashing their bodies with it. Folks killing themselves over money. They say, where your treasure is, that's where your heart is too. Luther and his mama didn't have much money or much of anything else, but they made out all right. Luther never went to bed hungry. Of course, he didn't always get to eat everything he liked, but he never starved, you can best believe that.

To everybody else, the Depression meant times of economic hardship. But Luther was battling his own kind of depression. Seems like Luther was always having trouble with women. How anybody nine years old could manage that, was beyond me. My main concern in life around that time, was figuring out my next strategy in the marble game with the fellas the next day. But then, I think Luther's been an old man just about all his life.

Luther was sitting on the steps in front of Jake Phillips' barber shop. Jake was the town barber and owned the Coolidge Savings & Loan then. He had other folks working for him. Still, he went around wearing his white cotton shirt with the sleeves rolled up, and waddling around in his brown corduroy pants and black suspenders. Jake never put on airs, but he was an ornery old codger as far as a lot of folks were concerned. He stood no more than 5'3", but hardly a soul would tangle with him, because he could be vicious when he wanted to. Somebody done him wrong, he was patient, biding his time until he could get back at him. I guess that's why black folks avoided him much as possible.

It was four in the afternoon. Folks were making their way over to the Trading Post to see what new stuff Bert had gotten in. Luther frowned when his nose detected a truck carrying a load of hogs through town. He rubbed his eyes from the dust flying in the air. Jake had spotted Luther's hung-down head from inside the shop. He slammed the screen door.

"Hey, what you doing there, boy?" Jake called, in the sternest voice he could find.

Luther was startled. It had been so quiet inside, he thought nobody was there. "Oh, I'm sorry—I was just—"

Jake grinned at him. "Now calm down. You ain't hurt nothing." He looked Luther up and down. "Hmmm—look like you could use a sody pop. What you say?"

Luther nodded and followed Jake inside. Luther didn't tell Jake he'd already had three of them at the Dairy Queen on the way from school.

Jake went over to the icebox as Luther looked around the barber shop. He told me he could never get over how neat and clean the place looked. He reckoned it had an alcohol-soap kind of smell. The hardwood floor looked like you could roll around on it in your Sunday-go-to-meeting clothes and still look good enough to go on to church. There were three black leather chairs with silver metal backings and legs. On the counters were razors and scissors and combs. There was a black vinyl-topped card table in the corner for the regulars, with a few clean, round metal ashtrays stacked on top. Luther noticed a few certificates on the wall. One of them he could make out was a notary public certificate. It was issued to Jake Immanuel Phillips, March 14, 1930. The mirrors sparkled and Luther could see Jake's bony figure standing behind him, smiling. Jake's small mouth full of tobacco-stained tiny teeth seemed to beg for more chewing space.

"I hope you like root beer, that's all I got." Jake said, handing the pop to Luther.

Luther's face lit up. Root beer was his favorite. "Thanks, Mista Phillips."

Jake scrunched up his small face and his cheekbones almost touched the corner of his light green eyes. "Now don't be cussing at me like that," Jake told him.

"Huh?" Luther was dumbfounded.

Jake pointed one of his small bony fingers at Luther. "My name's Jake. You got that?"

"Okay," Luther said, uneasily. He didn't know how his mama was gonna feel about that. She always taught him not to call grown folks by their first names.

Jake pulled out two of the chairs from the card table and motioned for Luther to sit down. Luther obeyed. Jake crossed one of his bony legs on top of the other. He looked even smaller when he was sitting down.

"You Kathryn's young 'un, ain't you?"

Luther's eyes grew wide. "You know my mama?"

Jake shrugged. "I know everybody. I suppose you don't remember me, do you?"

Luther shook his head.

"Nope, I guess you wouldn't. You was still in diapers when I left for Texas. I was always back and forth from Atlanta to Houston to New Orleans—on business and such."

Luther reckoned Jake was sizing him up.

"So how old you be about now?"

Luther had to think for a minute.

Jake cocked his head to one side. "Now I know you was born, not hatched—"

"I'll be ten tomorrow."

"Oh, a birthday boy! Umm, February twelfth, huh? A whole decade. Looks like you getting up there. Got a job yet?"

"Uh-uh."

Jake screwed up his face and his almond-shaped eyes tightened. "Boy, ain't nobody ever told you talking got more to it than questions and uh-huhs and uh-uhs?"

Luther started to nod. He looked up at Jake.

Jake grinned and then took out a stogie from his shirt pocket. "You know I'm just funning with you, don't you?"

Luther shook his head.

Jake let out a sigh. "Well, I am." His voice got softer. "So, how's your mama feeling? Ain't seen much of her lately."

"Doc says she's as good as she's gone be. She's in a lot of pain, though."

Jake took a deep breath and then coughed. "That what ailing you?"

"Some, I guess."

"Well, don't worry 'bout it. She's in mighty good hands."

Luther watched Jake puff on his stogie. The smell was familiar to him. It tickled his nose. "I guess so," Luther said. "But that's not what I was thinking 'bout just now. In fact I was sitting out there thinking and thinking, until I think I'm just about all thunk up."

"Boy, what you got to think so hard about 'sides your mama?" Jake asked.

Luther didn't answer right away. He could feel his face starting to get hot.

Jake flashed his tobacco stains. "Um-hmm, just as I thought—womenfolk."

Luther couldn't help but blink.

"Don't be surprised," Jake said. "You don't get to be my age and cain't recognize what women trouble look like on a boy's face."

Luther wondered just how old Jake was. Jake's reddish-brown hair had sprinkles of white in it. But his mama looked older than Jake, and she was only thirty-four.

"You don't look old to me," Luther said.

"Didn't say nothing about old. Just said, my *age.*" Jake stared down at him. "Go on, I know you dying to ask."

Luther put his head down. His mama told him it wasn't polite to go around asking grown folks how old they were.

"I'm forty-two," Jake said, proudly. "And I can still tangle with the best of 'em."

Luther watched him gulp down the last of his soda. Seemed like he drank the whole thing in about three swallows.

"Womenfolk," Jake said, propping his thin leg up on the wooden crates with empty pop bottles. "What else can drive a man to drink?"

Luther giggled and sipped his soda. He was feeling real comfortable talking to Jake.

"So, what's this lil' gal's name?" Jake asked him.

"Mary Ann."

"Pretty name. She pretty as her name?"

Luther nodded and his face turned red. "Except she has me all confused and puzzled most of the time."

"Why sho', boy, that's they job," Jake said. "Like my daddy used to say: they'll make you more confused than a porcupine in a cabbage patch."

Luther giggled. "Mary Ann loves to talk. She loves to talk a lot." He looked over at Jake. "How come girls talk so much, Mista Phillips?"

Jake sent him a look.

Luther remembered. "Oh, I . . . I mean, Jake. Why is it?"

Jake took his stogie out of his mouth and rubbed his chin. "It's in they genes."

Luther started to tell him that Mary Ann didn't wear jeans— just those pretty dresses with the white duck collars.

But Jake's eyes had started to glaze. He was in one of his "life according to Jake Phillips" modes. "Women is always fussing about who is more important: men or women. One of 'em even tried to tell me that women was more important because men is born out of women. Hmph, the way I figure it, God had to make men first and women-folk last. 'Cause if he'd a made women first, they'd a spent so much time talking, he'd a never got around to creating nothing else."

Luther almost choked on his soda. Some of it came out through his nose.

Jake gave him a pat on the back and kept on talking. "And, he'd a needed the other six days just to rest up."

Luther decided he liked Jake. He couldn't understand why folks said he was so ornery. He'd heard bad stories about Jake, but he'd never seen him do anything wrong. But then he reckoned he usually saw mostly good in folks, anyway.

"Yep," Jake said, concluding his theory, "you have to be careful with womenfolk. Cain't be giving your heart to just any woman."

Luther remembered the Hearts and Flowers Picnic they were having at school next week. Bo had told him that Mary Ann wanted him to sit next to him at the picnic, but Mary Ann wanted Luther to ask her. Luther couldn't figure out why he had to ask *her* when she was the one who wanted to do the sitting. But Luther had asked her anyway that day. Things didn't turn out too well.

"Jake—," Luther said, mustering up his nerve.

Jake pushed his stogie to one side. "Yep?"

"I need your advice on something."

"Let her rip."

"I got so nervous with Mary Ann today, that I think I mighta said the wrong thing, 'cause she got real mad at me."

"Hmph, with womenfolk you can be putting your life on the line just by saying hello, if they ain't in the mood for it. So, what you say that got her all riled up?"

"I said, 'Mary Ann, if you wanna sit next to me at the picnic, I won't make you move.'"

Jake laughed and slapped his knee. "Woo boy, I take it she didn't like that none."

"Uh-uh. So we just sat on the swings for a few more minutes, not saying nothing. Then she says, 'Luther, do you wanna sit next to me at the picnic or not?'" Luther looked at Jake. "Thought that was what I just said. So I said, 'yeah.' Then she put her hand on her hip and said, 'Luther, do you like me?' Luther told Jake how he shook his head. "If I didn't like her, I'd make her move if she sat next to me, right?"

"Right."

"So, I told her I liked her about as much as I like Big Ben."

"Big Ben?"

"My bullfrog."

Jake sat snickering and shaking his head.

"She didn't like that neither," Luther said. "Jake, I really like Big Ben a lot. But Mary Ann got all mad at me again. Told me she wouldn't sit next to me at the picnic or nowhere else, even if her life depended on it! And she said she's not gonna speak to me no more."

Jake let out a deep sigh. "Well, one of these days you gonna find that ain't so bad."

"Well, I don't know what's worse: having Mary Ann talking all the time, or not having her talk at all."

Jake smiled and his green eyes sparkled. He took out his stogie and blew a few smoke clouds. "Let me tell you a few things 'bout womenfolk. First of all, they say things they don't mean, they cries when they happy, and they gets they feelings hurt when you forget stuff like anniversaries, birthdays, and Ground Hog's Day and other such nonsense." Jake smacked his lips matter-of-factly. "But let me tell you a secret. I found that no matter how old they is, and no matter what size they is, womenfolk love poetry."

Luther looked up. "Poetry?"

"Yep—works every time. And I'm willing to bet it'll work with that there Mary Ann."

"But I ain't never wrote no poetry."

Jake patted him on the back. "You and your mama Kathryn goes to church every Sunday, don't you?"

"Yeah," Luther said, except he knew his mama hadn't been to church for months. Nobody from the church even came to visit or see how she was.

"Reads that Bible a lot, I take it?" Jake said.

"Yeah—but what's that—?"

Jake stood up. "Now I don't know about all that other stuff in there, and I ain't saying I believe it and all, but them Psalms and Proverbs—probably some of the best poetry there is."

Luther knew the Twenty-third Psalm by heart. His mama had told him to memorize it and say it whenever he felt afraid or alone. "You think that'll help me?" he asked, blinking his dark-brown eyes.

"Hmph, couldn't hurt. And looks like you in 'bout as deep as it gets." Jake winked his green eyes. "And you can take that to the bank and cash it."

Luther looked puzzled.

"Just an expression, boy. Just an expression."

Luther got up. "Thanks, Jake. Guess I better be getting home. Mama probably wondering where I been." He placed his empty bottle in the crate and started to leave.

"Hey, hold off a minute," Jake said. He rubbed his hairless chin. "You look like a baseball fan to me—"

Luther's eyes grew wide and he nodded. He held his breath as Jake went into the back room. He came out with an autographed picture of Ty Cobb. Luther couldn't believe Jake was handing it to him.

"Here, pin it up in your room. Next time you need some confidence, think about 'The Cobb.' Heck, that Mary Ann won't be able to resist you."

Luther's heart was doing somersaults several times. He looked down at the picture as if he'd been handed a pot of gold. "You mean—I can *have* it?"

Jake nodded. "Don't ask me how I come by it. Just know it's been good luck for me ever since I had it. And now I'm giving you some of my good luck. Plus, you did say it's your birthday tomorrow. Not every day a boy turns a whole decade." Jake put his hand on Luther's shoulder and knelt down like a coach. "Just remember: the next time you step up to bat with that lil' gal, watch what you say. You know, take the blood off the ball."

Luther smiled and thanked him. All the time he couldn't get anybody to trade him for a plain Ty Cobb baseball card, and there he was standing there with an *autographed* picture in his hands. He felt close to Jake. As they were leaving, he asked him why he never went to church.

Jake shrugged. "Ain't into being no hypocrite, like the rest of 'em in that place."

"Mama goes to church," Luther said.

"I don't mean your mama, boy. She's good people, your mama is. But the rest of 'em—Reverend Hayes included—" Jake started to finish and then shook his head. "It just ain't my cup of tea, that's all."

Luther stared at the floor and tightened his grip on the picture. "I like going to church."

Jake grabbed hold of his suspenders. "Now I ain't said nothing's wrong with liking church. Difference in you, your mama, and folks like you all, is your God meets you there 'cause you got spirit. Some of them others got as much spirit as this here cigar butt." Jake stabbed the butt into the ashtray until he put out the last of its embers. "The way I see it, a lot of folks pass judgment 'bout as fast as they pass gas. The trick is to stay out of the line of fire."

Luther snickered.

"Well anyhow," Jake said. "You read some of that poetry in your Bible. You'll come up with something."

That night Luther stayed up late. He gave his mama her pain killers and she finally fell asleep. He spent almost a whole hour trying to write a poem for Mary Ann. Nothing was coming to his mind, even after reading the Bible. Luther decided he needed more help.

He rolled off the bed onto his knees. "Please, God, I just got two favors. One of 'em you already know. I been asking for the last few months now. Can you please take Mama's pain away? Just heal her—somehow. And—you know I'm not good at this poetry stuff. But I'm tired of making a fool out of myself in front of Mary Ann. Lord, I just need a few words. It don't have to be nothing fancy. She ain't but ten years old. Thank you. Amen."

The next day at school, the teacher, Miss Parker, caught Luther passing his poem to Mary Ann. Luther forgot to add that part to this prayer.

"Mr. Rawlings!" she called out in her nasally, high-pitched voice. "Do you wish to read what's on that piece of paper to the rest of the class?"

"No, ma'am," Luther said. His face grew hotter as the class laughed.

"You know the rules, Luther," she insisted. "Anyone caught distributing notes in class, must do what?" She pursed her lips as Luther stared at the ground. "Must do what?" she repeated, louder this time.

"Read it to the whole class," Luther muttered.

Miss Parker nodded and folded her arms, knowing she'd won. Luther's hands started sweating and he could hear his heart pounding. He knew Miss Parker. She was like God when it came to rules. She made a rule, she stuck to it. Didn't change one stitch no matter who it was. Where was a good thunderstorm when he needed one?

Luther stood up, slowly unfolded the note and swallowed hard. He took one last look around the room. He wanted to remember what they looked like in case he never came back. Just his luck, though. Everybody, including Miss Parker, was staring right at him. Some of them started to giggle. Luther tried to read the poem as fast as he could. The only problem was he didn't know how to talk or read fast.

"Dear Mary Ann:
    God gave me a heart, to know how to love;
God gave me life, thru his Son above;
    I wish you could know him, then you could see
His love is greater than mine can be.
    P.S. Please sit next to me at the picnic.
Your friend, Luther B. Rawlings."

He flung himself down into his seat and didn't dare look up. Miss Parker was being awfully quiet. So he glanced up. She was smiling at him!

"And the 'B' stands for 'Bonehead!'" Bo yelled out. Some of the kids started laughing, but Miss Parker made them all be quiet. "Luther—" her voice was softer.

"Ma'am?"

"Now you know I still don't approve of passing notes in class—you know that?"

"Yes, ma'am."

"But . . . I think your poem was very nice. And I think Mary Ann is very lucky to have you as a friend."

Luther told me he was speechless.

"And if she won't sit next to you at the picnic, I will."

No offense against Miss Parker, but Luther was glad Mary Ann sat next to him instead of his teacher. He would have been the laughing stock of the whole school. It was bad enough he'd have to get over them calling him the Picnic Poet. He was glad though that

Mary Ann didn't seem to mind that he snuck Big Ben along for extra company.

Some months later Mary Ann's family moved to Los Angeles. She wrote to Luther for a time about how exciting Hollywood was and that she was going to be an actress one day. Luther would answer every letter, but after a while the letters stopped. Luther was sure he was through with womenfolk for a while. He decided he'd devote all his time to the most important woman in his life: his mama, Kathryn.

Luther admired his mama. She could do just about anything with her hands like knitting, sewing and crocheting. She could even do more with a brush and watercolors than some folks could do with twenty brushes and a hundred oil paints. They say the camera don't lie. Kathryn's paintings didn't lie either. She had a knack for painting faces. She could paint somebody down to the smallest detail—every wrinkle, every scar—after meeting them only one time. She was the only woman who could look you straight in the eye and not blink until you did. Luther tried to stare her down one time. Didn't make it. Luther said she had more concentration than Lefty Grove and Walter Johnson at the pitcher's mount.

Kathryn died the year after Coolidge's Patriotic Week. My mama had called it a "female disease." Luther said it was cancer. She had suffered a long time. Luther found out she'd been hiding how bad off she'd gotten. He thought she was getting better because she didn't ask him to bring her medicine to her anymore. It was at the arts and crafts exhibition that Luther first recognized something was seriously wrong. His right eye had been itching and kind of watery that whole day, and he didn't know why.

Kathryn had entered one of the pictures she'd painted of Luther in the portrait contest. All day long folks kept saying, "Hey, you're that boy in the picture. Is she your mama?" Luther would tell them yes, and they'd go on and on to Kathryn about what great talent she had, and how Luther would probably have the same kind of talent one day. Kathryn would never respond, just manage a weak smile. She probably knew as soon as they got out of her sight their mouths would start gossiping about how she had Luther out of wedlock, and how she once had the "nasty woman's disease." It took Luther three weeks, searching through some of Doc's books and magazines to find out they were talking about gonorrhea. Wasn't anything nasty about his mama, Luther had insisted. I knew that. Had to be some man who gave it to her in the first place.

There was an unusual sadness in Kathryn's face that day. She was quiet as Luther talked about one day going to the World Series in New York. At first, he thought she was quiet because her painting didn't win the contest.

Luther gave her a big hug. "Yours was the best one there, Mama."

"Of course, Luther," she said softly. "Look what I had to work with." Her eyes were red and tired-looking. "I'm gonna lie down for a while. You gonna be all right?"

"Yeah, Mama, don't worry 'bout dinner, I'll make myself a sandwich."

Kathryn moved slowly back to her room with her elbow tucked in at her side. Luther had to do just about everything for her after that, since she eventually couldn't walk anymore.

Several months later, Luther sat listening to the Yankees game on the radio. He was busting with excitement because The Babe had broken his own home run record by hitting sixty home runs! Kathryn's screams drowned out his excitement. Luther said the last time he heard a screen like that was when they butchered that hog over at the Taylor's place. Luther ran in to her.

"Mama, let me call Doc."

"No, Luther—don't bother him—he's done what he can do."

How he hated watching his mama suffer like that. She placed her thin pale hand on his forehead. "Luther—listen to me—listen to me real good—" Her dark brown eyes had started to fade.

"Sometimes folks get sick—and they just don't get well—it's just God's way."

Luther knelt down and kissed her forehead. It was cold and sweaty. She needed something to cheer her up, he decided. He just knew God was going to answer his prayer. He shot out of there down the road to round up some of her favorite yellow and white daisies out of Old Doc Peterson's yard. Doc's wife, Beulah, yelled at Luther to get out of their garden, but he managed to pluck a bunch of them anyway. The way Luther saw it, it was the least Doc could do. All those years his mama cleaned his house, and the one time she needed his help he couldn't even cure her. But Kathryn never got to enjoy the flowers. They ended up on her grave instead.

Silently, Luther cursed God and his way. Why Mama? That question burned deep inside of him. He said if it had to be somebody, why not that man up in Prescott, the man who was supposed to be his father, who never came around to see if they were alive or dead? Luther knew he couldn't look a bit like that man—resembled his mama in every way, from her auburn hair, square face and pointy nose, down to her big bones and flat feet. Kathryn never talked much about Luther's daddy. Every time Luther would ask about him, she'd say, "Just pray for him, sweetie." Then she'd change the subject.

Kathryn didn't really leave enough to cover her funeral expenses. She had given Luther a coffee can under the bed, with forty dollars in it, all in one dollar bills, and a box of old keepsakes. But he made out all right. Jake picked up the slack, but he asked Luther to keep it quiet.

"What I do ain't none of them folks' business," Jake had insisted. But Luther couldn't understand why Jake chose to go out of town the day of Kathryn's funeral.

At the funeral Luther had looked around the church as Constance, Reverend Hayes' wife, was badly playing *Nearer My God To Thee*, Kathryn's favorite song, on the organ. He knew everybody there—the same people he'd seen Sunday after Sunday, except they still seemed like strangers to him. He and his mama had no living relatives that Luther knew of. Kathryn was an only child. She told him she grew up in an orphanage in Texas because her parents gave her up for adoption. She moved to Arizona when she grew up. Seems Doc Peterson's brother worked at the orphanage and recommended her for the job as Doc's housekeeper.

With Kathryn gone, it was a good thing Luther looked older than he was. Luther was just turning thirteen. Some of the folks would say, "He's got to be at least seventeen or eighteen." He just decided to never tell them anything different. So he figured it wasn't really lying.

Luther had to quit school, but he read everything he could get his hands on. He had a love for words. Shoot, he even ended up teaching me a few things. He managed to round up all kinds of odd jobs: taking care of yards, running errands for Jake in the barber shop, tending horses and shining shoes. Folks used to pass by and shake their heads: "What a shame," they said, "having to shine shoes—a nice white boy like that."

Luther figured he'd work on trying to find out just what kind of work nice white boys like him was supposed to be doing, but for then he was happy just to be working and getting paid.

For a long time I wanted to talk to Luther and ask him to come work with me blacksmithing. But my mama told me the time wasn't right. She said folks' hearts still wasn't in the right place. Didn't seem right to me, even at that time. Living in the same town with white folks—know just about everyone of them, breathe the same air, eat the same kind of food—and still couldn't be friends with them or sit next to them in public without getting thrown in jail. I asked my mama when it was going to be time. She just gave me one of her saucy looks, closed her eyes, and said, "Chile, believe me, we'll know."

Jake Phillips had the same idea I did. He didn't take too kindly to the way folks pitied Luther, so he let him shine shoes inside his barber shop. Luther liked the friendly atmosphere inside, and the way everybody kept Jake up on what was going on in town.

"Jake, I'm gonna own a barber shop just like this one day," Luther told him. Jake would just shine those green eyes at him and push his cigar to one side. "And I'm through with women for good," Luther insisted.

Jake scrunched up his face. He put down his scissors. Told Bert from the Trading Post to excuse him. He took Luther over in the back. "What's this foolishness?" Jake said. "You ain't going funny on me, are you?"

"Naw, Jake. It's just—"

Jake bit his lip. "You seem to keep getting hurt all the time. That it?"

"Yeah. Seems like they keep leaving me. Mary Ann left and stop writing to me. I kinda liked Willa Mae, Mary Ann's cousin, for a while. Remember?"

"Yeah, I remember that one too," Jake said, smiling.

Luther sighed, "She quit me for Bo."

Jake listened and puffed on his stogie.

"Now, Jake, I could take all of that. But this . . . this is just too much. A mama's not supposed to leave you—well, at least not this soon, anyway."

"I know, boy. I know." Jake rubbed his chin. "But it ain't gone always be like that." There was a slight crack in his voice. "Everybody feels lonely, boy. Dying is part of living. I know that's hard to hear. But it's a fact of life. You just have to go on with yours. Just keep the good memories down off in your heart. Folks always stay alive inside your heart, if you want 'em to." Then he gave Luther a friendly pat on the back and winked his green eyes.

Luther was glad to have Jake around. He'd learned that not all of his prayers were going to be answered. At least, not like he thought they'd be. But he prayed anyway that Jake would always be there.

Chapter Three

It had been a little more than four years since Hoover had been defeated in 1932. Folks blamed him for the Depression, for some reason. Jake told Luther and me that Hoover had made political points when he was in office by buying the first movie ticket from Mary Pickford, to help support the motion picture industry's benefit performance. It was supposed to "lighten the burdens of desolate households all over the country," the newspaper said. When they got through, my mama said our household was just as desolate as when they started. But "Frankie D" (as we called Roosevelt) had been planning his "New Deal" when Luther was just starting puberty. But like I said, I think Luther's been old all of his life.

If folks had known Luther was only thirteen, they'd have had a fit. The white folks thought *I* was eighteen, and I just two years older than Luther. I was doing real good learning to take over my daddy's blacksmithing business when he retired. I had no idea somebody was gonna give him an early retirement to his grave that year.

My daddy, Willie Jackson, was a tall, wry black man with a crooked smile. The smile fit because he was a hand mucker when it came to cards. He'd hide cards in his overalls and switch them with the ones he got dealt, most of the time without folks knowing what he was doing. I guess it was only a matter of time before it caught up with him. It was the following week that Luther and me got to know each other.

I spotted Luther in Jake's truck just as it ran out of gas. The tank was on "E" and Luther forgot to fill up before he left Casa Grande. I watched him jump out and start trudging in the dirt, gas can in his hand, scratching his head. It was the end of December— pretty cool outside and six miles into town. I pulled my truck up beside him. Luther was scared to look at me. I saw him looking around to see if anybody else was around. Wasn't a soul within miles.

"Well, if it ain't Mr. Shoe Shine," I called to him. "Got a problem?" Luther held up the gas can, still not looking at me. "Need a lift?" I asked. Luther hesitated and was still looking around. He nodded. "Jump in," I said.

Luther came around and jumped in as fast as he could, and closed the door. He still wouldn't look at me. He set the gas can on his lap. I reached over in my ashtray compartment and pulled out one of the chocolates that I'd cut up into small pieces and wrapped in tinfoil. I offered it to Luther. He shook his head and fidgeted in his seat. I unwrapped the chocolate and stuffed it in my mouth.

"Where you on your way to?" I asked him, trying to strike up a conversation to calm him down.

He was still leaning forward, looking straight ahead like he was the one driving. "I was running an errand for Jake. Had to go up to Hattie's for some supplies."

The chocolate was sticking to all the silver in my mouth, making it harder for me to talk. "I meant to tell you how sorry we all were—you know—about your mama passing away just a few years ago."

Luther turned to look at me. I noticed he was growing hair on his face now. "That's real nice of you, Hawk. Thank you."

I smiled. "So you know my name, huh?"

Luther leaned back in the seat. "Yeah, everybody knows big Hawk Williams. You and your daddy—" I could tell it just occurred to Luther. "Oh, Hawk, I'm sorry—"

I shrugged. "It's all right."

"Don't you miss him?" Luther asked. I wanted to say he wasn't my real daddy, but I decided against it. The truth was my mama was pregnant with me when she married Willie Jackson. I always wondered why Mama Lucille gave me her maiden name, Williams, instead of Jackson, like Willie. Mama told me she was born with that name and wasn't about to change it for no man, no matter how many times she got married. Willie was Mama's third husband. I shrugged my shoulders again.

"Well," Luther went on, "at least you had your daddy around to raise you. That man supposed to live up in Prescott somewhere, but I don't really know where he is."

"That man?" I asked.

"One supposed to be my daddy."

I noticed the rows and rows of cotton out in Sheriff Hickerwood's fields. "I take it you don't know him?" I asked.

Luther shook his head. "Uh-uh. Not even his name."

"Why don't you just go up there and ask around. Somebody got to know something about him."

Luther shook his head. "Nothing doing."

I glanced over at him. "Why not?"

Luther shrugged, and stretched out his long legs. "It's 'cause I got a strong feeling he knows where I am, even if I don't."

I laughed. Luther gave me a look. Then he grinned when he realized what he'd said.

He was quiet for a few moments, and then looked down at the gas can. "Hope you don't mind me asking," he blurted out, "but I heard they found your daddy's body up in Payson last week." I nodded, and Luther went on. "They said he was cheating at Tonk." Luther looked up at me like I was gonna hit him or something.

I let out a big sigh and stuffed another piece of chocolate in my mouth. "You heard right. Willie Jackson was a damn good blacksmith, but he had the morals of a jackal." I sat up in my seat and gripped the wheel with both hands. "They found him tied up in the trunk of Jake's brand new Roadster." I bit my lip. "It takes

29

somebody with a sick and twisted mind to kill somebody—cut off his manhood—and then stuff it down his throat to gag him—and then just leave him there to bleed to death." I could feel the chocolate coming back up. I pulled off to the side of the road and opened the door. I spewed out everything in me.

When I was done, Luther handed me his handkerchief. "I . . . I'm sorry, Hawk. I can walk the rest of the way if you want."

I shook my head. "I'm all right." I tried to smile as I handed the handkerchief back to him. "Guess it's not good to keep things down inside too long." I noticed Luther had set the gas can on the floor. I started the truck and looked straight ahead. "He was my step-daddy."

Luther smiled. "That mean you probably don't have the same kind of morals."

I nodded.

"Good," Luther said, "'cause I play a mean game of Tonk—for fun, of course." He looked at me. "You know—one of these days . . ."

I nodded and took off down the road.

Luther fidgeted in his seat again. "Hawk, I know folks been saying Jake Phillips and your . . . Willie . . . never got along . . . you know . . . that Jake was always accusing him of cheating at cards and fooling around with Velma . . ." He looked over at me. Velma was the Court Clerk. She had skin almost as white as ivory soap. Sometimes she even smelled like ivory soap. I wasn't sure how old she was, but I know she had to be at least ten years younger than Jake. I didn't say a word. "But I know Jake didn't kill him. I just know it," Luther insisted.

"That colored orphan asylum just celebrated a hundred years," I said, matter-of-factly.

"Huh?" Luther said, taken aback. "Oh—yeah—okay. But, like I said, you don't know Jake like I do."

"President Roosevelt just gave orders to build two new battleships," I reported again.

Luther looked puzzled. Then he formed his mouth to say "Jake?" I narrowed my brow and looked over at him. "Old Farmer's Almanac for 1937 is ready. You can send for it anytime now."

Luther settled back in his seat. "Cloudy, light showers expected throughout the day," he said, and then looked over at me. We both laughed.

I could see Shope's in the distance, so I pulled over. "I think this is where we better part company," I told him. "For now."

Luther nodded. He surprised me and reached over and shook my hand. "Thanks, Hawk."

I sat there for a few minutes and waited until he was almost coming upon Shopes. Then I drove on into town, passing right by him. Neither one of us looked each other's way.

You would have thought church was the last place for segregation. Not so. I don't know about Reverend Ward's Coolidge Community Church. Never been there, but Reverend Hayes' First Southern Baptist Church of Zion thought they were liberal. Black folks and white folks could all praise the Lord together, except we had to sit in different sections. Luther sat close to the front in the section marked "Whites Only."

Constance Hayes, the Reverend's wife, played the organ. Sheriff Hickerwood was the deacon and sat up in the pulpit with Reverend Hayes. I sat with my mama Lucille, my Aunt Mabel, the rest of the Jacksons, the Taylors, the Stewarts and the Johnsons. There were more of us than them, which is why our section was always too crowded, while they had at least two rows vacant every week.

Luther and me got to know each other real good. But we didn't want to arouse any suspicion, so we worked out signals to use in church. Coughs and sneezes meant "I'll meet you at the swamp to listen to the ball game." Eye-rubs and head scratching meant "I have to spend Sunday afternoon with my family," and hand-clapping and toe-tapping—if it was me—meant "I'll meet you at the hole for bass fishing. If it was Luther—it meant he was probably off-beat again.

For at least three months my mama kept thinking I was coming down with the flu. She'd see me coughing and sneezing or rubbing my eyes, and start feeling my forehead to see if I had a temperature. Luther and me almost hurt ourselves trying to keep from laughing. I heard Aunt Mabel whisper to my mama, "Lue, I'm so glad that boy is finally starting to like church." By that time, though, my mama knew something was up, but she never let on. She just gave me a knowing kind of warning out the corner of her eye, as if to say, "I know what you up to—just don't get caught."

Four years later Luther and me did get caught. Me, by the draft board; Luther, by Amanda Beaumont. The army threw me back when they found out I had diabetes. Luther said that was the only thing Amanda and me had in common. Seems like the Japanese attacking Pearl Harbor was nothing compared to the trouble Luther was headed for. Trouble of the worst kind: the marrying kind.

Amanda was only sixteen, but she was tall for a white girl her age. She used to look Luther right in the eye when she wore her heels. Had her mama's looks: long red hair and eyes as blue as Coolidge Dam, a long thin nose that turned downward when she smiled, and a thin mouth with fire-red lips. She and Luther met for the first time when he accidentally walked her home.

Luther had spotted Amanda walking home with her other friends one afternoon after school. They usually passed by Jake's barber shop every school day. Luther would always pick that time to sweep the porch outside. Seemed like Amanda got his routine down real well, and Luther knew she saw him staring at her. She'd be talking with her friends, and soon as she caught sight of Luther she'd nudge one of them and nod Luther's way.

That day they all started giggling at Luther, who didn't see what was so funny. He decided that was enough sweeping for one day and went inside to put the broom back in the storage closet.

When he got inside, Doc Peterson, Sam, Bert and some of the other fellas started snickering. Jake sent them a hush-up look and made a motion to Luther. Luther looked puzzled. Jake demonstrated on himself, as if he was zipping his fly. Luther's face turned red. He went into the back where the storage closet was. He was there for a good while. Jake came back where he was, wiping his hands on his apron.

"It ain't nothing to worry about, boy," Jake told Luther. "That bunch of uncouth no-accounts in there—there ain't a one of 'em this ain't happened to before. Don't let 'em get the best of you."

Luther hung his head. "But she seen it too," he said.

Jake rubbed his chin. "That lil' gal you kind of sweet on that keeps passing by here every day?" he asked.

Luther looked at him.

Jake grinned. "Sorry, boy, but you ain't got no secrets. Specially after today."

Luther fidgeted.

"You just better find some other way of letting that lil' gal know how much you like her," Jake added, "'cause they can put you in jail for such things."

Luther's eyes got wide. "Jail!"

"Now don't get excited. It's what you might call a minor infraction." He pointed to Luther's crotch. "I think they call it indecent exposure."

Luther's face was redder than that barber pole outside by then.

Jake put his hand on Luther's shoulder. "Oh, don't worry about it, boy. Maybe that lil' gal liked what she seen." He laughed and started to leave.

"Jake?"

"Yeah?"

"You think she'd go out with me?"

Jake's green eyes twinkled. "Only one way to find out."

On Friday, Jake Phillips let Luther off early. Luther knew he was going to have to move quick, otherwise he'd have to wait another week to ask Amanda out. When he saw her and her friends coming way down the road, he hid behind one of the huge beer barrels across from Sam's Tavern. Luther was amused at how Amanda kept looking around for him. She seemed disappointed when she didn't see him. He liked that.

Luther followed them, trying his best to keep out of sight. He watched as one by one Amanda said 'bye to her friends. She towered over all three of them. Amanda lived quite a ways from Jake's shop. That's when Luther realized she'd been intentionally taking the long way home. He noticed she was headed down Galveston Road, where some of the wealthy folks lived.

When Luther turned the corner, he didn't see her any more. He knew she had long legs but she must've been walking like the devil. Like to scared Luther silly when she jumped out from behind a tree!

"Boo!" she yelled, and started giggling when she saw him jump. Luther couldn't find his voice. Amanda eyed him real suspicious like. "Are you following me?"

Luther was going to shake his head, and then looked at the ground. Amanda cocked her head to one side and then twirled a strand of her red hair. "Who are you, anyway?" she asked him.

Luther's cheeks were on fire. "I'm Luther."

Amanda eyed him. "You always go around stalking people?"

"I wasn't stalking you," Luther said, turning to leave.

She got in front of him and folded her arms. "Oh no? Well, if you wanted to know where I lived, how come you didn't just ask me?"

Luther shrugged, but still couldn't look at her. He had the strangest feeling. He wanted to stay and he wanted to run—all at the same time. Amanda played with the red locket of hair around her neck. "And in case you didn't know, my name is Amanda Beaumont." She stuck out her hand. Luther hesitated. She looked hurt and her manner changed. "Well, Luther Whatever, I don't have all day to talk. I've got to get home." She turned, and her long red hair flared down around her shoulders.

"Rawlings!" Luther blurted out, walking behind her. "That's my name—Luther Rawlings." He stuck out his sweaty palm. "Glad to meet you—Miss Beaumont."

Her eyes softened as she took his hand. Luther's hands started to sweat again. "Well," Amanda said, smiling. "I guess *I should* thank you for walking me home." Her teeth were so white against her red lips. It reminded Luther of a layer of the barber pole at Jake's.

Luther walked beside her until they came to a big red-brick house with a china berry tree in front of it. They both stood there for a few moments not knowing what to say. Luther couldn't seem to get the lump out of his throat. He looked through the gate and saw a man with thick eyebrows and beady eyes peeping out the window.

Amanda followed his look. "That's papa," she told him. "He's so nosy. But that's what makes him such a good judge, I guess."

Luther's mouth dropped open. "He's a judge?"

"Yeah, but he should have been a district attorney. He's forever cross-examining me." Amanda smiled. "He's my papa, and I love him."

Luther kept watching Mr. Beaumont watching them. "He probably waiting for you to come in," Luther said.

"Yeah," Amanda said. "So, where you from, Luther?"

He felt uncomfortable talking in front of her gate with her daddy watching. "I'm from here."

Amanda crossed her feet. She was wearing long white socks and black patent leather shoes with straps across. "We moved here from Nevada."

"Oh," was all Luther could say.

"You like movies?" Amanda asked him.

"Huh? Oh, sure, I like movies." He tried to act casual. "I go all the time."

"There's a double feature playing in Casa Grande tomorrow evening," she said. "*Coast Guard* and *Pioneer Trail*."

Luther's insides were doing somersaults like they did whenever he was asked to a ball game.

"See you over here at 5:30," Amanda said, without missing a beat.

Luther nodded. "Okay."

"You can drive papa's car. He won't mind."

Luther hesitated. "Um—if it's all the same to you—I'd like to drive my own car."

Amanda blinked. "You have a car?"

Luther knew he'd made some more points. "Well, kind of. I'm saving up to buy that truck of Jake Phillips. He's my boss. He lets me drive it from time to time."

"Well, all right," Amanda said, smiling.

Luther felt sure he was finally learning how to handle women. He and Amanda dated regular after that. Sometimes Luther would pay, sometimes she would pay. Luther always felt uncomfortable about Amanda paying, but she was headstrong and insisted.

"That way I don't feel obligated to you," she told him. She made him promise not to tell her daddy about it, though. Amanda's beady-eyed daddy was over-protective of her. He made it clear by what he *didn't* say that he didn't approve of Luther, no matter how honorable Luther's intentions were.

Luther felt uncomfortable whenever he visited Amanda. Even though Mr. Beaumont answered the door and stared at Luther every time, like he didn't know why Luther was there, Mrs. Beaumont would come to the rescue and ask him to come in. He could tell the Beaumonts had money and were not afraid to show it. Everything was decorated in the style of Louis XVI. Luther was afraid to sit on the sofa. He said it looked too delicate for comfort. The hardwood floor smelled like lemon, and Luther reckoned he could see himself in it. A battleship inside a glass bottle sat on top of a black and gold marble table. Luther kept wondering how Mr. Beaumont managed that.

Mrs. Beaumont was always nice to Luther. She looked like an older version of Amanda, except she was short and seemed more fragile. Amanda had her daddy's tall stature. Luther dreaded what seemed like eternity as Mrs. Beaumont went to get Amanda. He was left hanging on the end of the mohair sofa as Mr. Beaumont examined him with his legs crossed and his pipe between his teeth.

Mr. Beaumont would ask Luther a different version of the same question every time. "What are your intentions toward Mandy?" or "Have you been married before?" or "How many girlfriends do you have?" Luther wondered what he would say if he found out it was always Amanda who kept pushing to have relations with him. He was sure Mr. Beaumont would have swallowed his pipe.

After a few years of dating Luther had finally paid Jake for the truck. He and Amanda sat parked about a mile out of town. Amanda had a temper when she didn't get her way, and she pouted her cherry lips at him.

"What's the matter with you anyway, Luther Rawlings? Don't you love me?"

"Course I do, Manda." That's what he called her. "It's just—it's not *time* yet, that's all."

"Luther, I think your clock is much too slow. It's been several years now. I'm almost eighteen and you close to nineteen. We are consenting adults."

"Well, maybe you consenting, but I'm not consenting to nothing right now, Manda. It just don't seem right."

Amanda grit her teeth. "Sometimes I swear, Luther, you act like you about forty years old!"

"Well, Manda, what about your mama and daddy? What they gone say?"

She tossed the curls she was wearing in her head. "They won't say a word 'cause they won't be here. That is, unless you plan on inviting them."

Luther's face grew red. "Manda, the things you say!"

"Oh don't be such a fuddy duddy." She had a hurt look on her face. She turned toward the door on the passenger side, her back to Luther. Luther knew he was going to have to speed up his clock. He rubbed her shoulder. She flinched. "Please, Manda, don't be mad at me. The truth is I never slept with nobody before."

"What?" Amanda asked.

Luther shrugged. "Now I know your daddy don't approve of me none 'cause I work in a barber shop. I know he rather you marry some rich fella come from a well-to-do family with blue-blood relatives—" Amanda was quiet. "—but things don't always turn out the way we think they should. All I know is I love you a lot, Manda, and I'm ready to get married tonight if we have to— that is, providing you wanna marry up with somebody like me."

Amanda's eyes looked like Hoover Dam the time it flooded over. She clutched Luther so tight and kissed him, that he couldn't breathe. She let him go for air, sobbed some more, and then went to hugging him some more. When she finally let Luther catch his breath, he drove her back home and walked her to the door. She never did stop crying. She kissed Luther some more.

"Manda," Luther said softly.

"Yes . . . Luther?" she said, sniffing.

"Does this mean, yes?"

"Oh, Luther!" she said, shaking her head. "Of course it means yes." She hugged him and Luther squeezed her tight. He knew Mr. Beaumont was not going to peep out the window. Amanda had threatened to stop speaking to him if he kept doing it. So he leaned over and planted a kiss on her lips.

"Oh, I love you so much," Amanda told him.

Luther went home that night and came knocking on my door. He was on top of the world. I tried not to put a damper on his party, but I asked him how Mr. Beaumont felt about it. Luther said he knew her daddy was going to give them some trouble, but Amanda told him she had a plan. He said she promised to take care of everything. But Luther wasn't ready for what Amanda had planned.

"Elope ?" Luther said, when Amanda told him the next day.

"Come on, Luther, you know it's the only way. Why, we can even have fun in Las Vegas."

Luther shook his head. "Oh no, Manda. That's gangster town. Any and everything goes on there. Folks are always ending up dead, or something."

Amanda giggled. "Don't be so silly. Those are just stories. I lived there—remember?"

Luther took her hand. "But Manda, in a gambling city—that's not where I want to get married."

Amanda snuggled up next to him. "You know how papa is." She grabbed Luther around the waist. "And once we're *already* married, what can papa say? We can have a big church wedding later on."

"Well, all right," Luther said at last. "But that means Hawk has to be my best man."

Amanda's mouth fell open. "Hawk Williams? But I thought you were going to ask Jake Phillips?"

Luther nodded. "Yeah, I know, but Jake's not gonna be in town next week. He's got some business to take care of."

Amanda poked out her lips. "But, Luther, what are people going to think?"

"I don't know, Manda. But Hawk's my best friend—next to Jake."

Amanda stared at him and sighed. "Okay, but when we have the real wedding, Jake is the best man."

Luther nodded.

He was slow about things, but Amanda didn't hesitate on anything. She took care of all the paperwork. I knew she wasn't too thrilled about me. I could tell the folks at *The Doves of Happiness* chapel in Las Vegas weren't either. But Luther was already prepared for any objections. If I didn't know better, I'd swear that simpleton act of his was just that: an act. He could be shrewd when you least expected it. He'd given me the five dollars and told me to say I was paying for the wedding. It worked. They had "hemmed" and "hawed" for a while, but I guess they figured it didn't matter what color my skin was, as long as my money was green.

That was the quickest wedding I ever saw. There was some sorry music, a few "do you takes," some "I do's," and boom, they were married! I could tell Luther was devastated.

"Not at all what I expected," he told me later.

"Sure hope your marriage lasts a whole lot longer," I told him.

"Well, Amanda's my wife. She's happy and that makes me happy," Luther said.

I could see the joy in his eyes and I gave him a hug. I had hugged Amanda, too, when they were pronounced man and wife. She was as stiff as a board. She never said much to me, and she never returned my smiles, but at least she never *said* anything unkind to me. I appreciated that at least.

I parked the truck in a secluded area, out of the way. My mama, Lucille, always cooked like she was feeding an army of folks. So, I was loaded up with a basket full of chicken. I was set for the next few hours. I stayed in there with the windows cracked and listened to the radio. I'd never been inside one of those casinos. Gambling was definitely something my mama didn't talk about and didn't allow anybody else to mention in her house, let alone participate in. I had to tell my mama, Lucille, what we were up to. She was so upset, she had to take one of her blood pressure pills before it was time.

"Now, you swear to me you ain't gone go in that place!" she yelled at me.

"Mama, I promise. Relax. They not gonna let no colored man in there, no how."

She settled down, and then her eyes lit up when she realized she had the scoop on some juicy gossip. She swore she'd keep the wedding a secret until after we got back. But I knew as soon as we left, *she* was probably getting calls to see if *she'd* heard the news about it.

I must've been asleep for a couple of hours. When I woke up, I drove back to the El Rancho Vegas Hotel. I saw Luther and Amanda, all flustered, and looking around for the truck. I pulled up to let them in. When they got in, I noticed Amanda was clutching onto her purse. She was strangely quiet. I say strange, because she had talked all the way up there earlier that day. I kept thinking she'd lost all their money or something. I could tell Luther was as confused as I was.

"Manda, I'm sorry our honeymoon was ruined," Luther finally said.

She looked over at him. "Luther, it wasn't ruined. It was fine, just fine." She snuggled over closer to Luther who was sitting in the middle of us. "Luther, you know I love you."

Luther's face reddened. "Manda, please . . ." He kept nudging his head over in my direction.

"Aw, I'm sure Hawk don't mind, do you?" I almost swerved the truck. She not only spoke directly to me, but she actually smiled at me.

"No, of course not. It's your honeymoon."

Amanda smiled and snuggled up closer to Luther. "See?" Apparently Amanda had some big news for Luther and was trying to wait until later, but I guess she couldn't hold it any longer.

As soon as were about five miles out, she started breathing real hard. "Manda, you all right?" Luther asked.

"Oh, Luther, I been sitting here praying that I'm not dreaming. I think I'm still in shock, actually—or maybe they made a mistake—I was afraid to say anything earlier—thinking they might come after us—"

I turned to Luther. "What in the world did you two do in there?"

Amanda waved her hand at me, as if to say don't worry, and then she turned to Luther. "We won—are you ready for this—*three thousand dollars!*"

"What?!" Both Luther and I said together.

Amanda nodded, still smiling. "That's what they gave us!"

Luther reached for her purse. "That can't be right, Manda. You must've counted wrong—you had to!"

Amanda waved her hands in the air and kissed the cross she was wearing. "Go ahead and check. It's three thousand any way you count it!" She was almost drunk with joy.

Luther finished counting and looked over at me. I saw the confirmation on his face. "Luther, what kind of gambling did you two do?" I asked him.

Luther shook his head. Mentally, he was trying to fit all the pieces of the puzzle together. I know he'd felt uneasy about going to a casino. He didn't like gambling, not even bingo—for money. He said there was so much noise inside. Bells and whistles going off like crazy, bright lights flashing everywhere. The place smelled like ashtrays dipped in toilet water. There were GI's everywhere. Seemed like everybody was wearing uniforms. The dealers looked like they had just come from the kitchen, Luther told me. They still had on their aprons.

Luther had watched two little old ladies with big noses and orthopedic shoes clutching oversized handbags. The two of them weren't talking to each other, but you could tell they were together by the way they would look over and smile at each other whenever the bell rang and coins would pour out. A petite, blonde-haired woman in a tight black skirt, white blouse two sizes too small, black silk stockings and black high heels, kept asking the two women if they wanted something to drink. They always nodded, and she kept bringing them Mai Tai's, and they kept winning coins and sticking them back into the slots as fast as they came out. Luther didn't see much point in the whole thing.

Amanda had fun, though. Luther told her they had thirty dollars to spend. She was real smart. She told Luther she had figured it out: she had six different things she wanted to play and she would spend five dollars on each one. She asked Luther if he wanted to take one of them.

"I don't think so," Luther replied.

"Oh, c'mon, Luther honey. How will you know if it's fun or not if you don't even try it?"

Luther shrugged. "Plus, it seems to me gambling's not how God intends for folks to be making a living."

Amanda cocked her head to one side. "Oh, Luther, we are not trying to make a profession out of this." Her voice grew softer. "It's . . . it's just fun. Why, just think how exciting it would be if you put your money on the roulette wheel and Number Three came up, hmmm?"

The crack of a smile appeared on Luther's face. "I guess a person could get excited about that."

Amanda snuggled next to him. "Just play the wheel with me a few times. If you don't like it, you can stop." Then she stroked his cheek and kissed him. "Besides, I'm Mrs. Luther Rawlings now. And you did say 'til death do us part—not gambling do us part."

Luther hugged her. "All right, you win. Let's go."

She grabbed his hand and they were off. Number Three never came up, and they lost all of the five dollars at the roulette wheel. Then, they ended up at the craps table. Luther was getting dizzy watching people dropping chips, rolling dice, dropping more chips and picking up chips. Amanda was trying to act like she'd been there hundreds of times. She put one of her chips down on the Field.

"That way you have lots of chances to win," she whispered to Luther.

Luther nodded and put one of his next to hers. Everybody seemed to hold their breaths as a hairy, heavy-set man, in a V-neck shirt and a tattoo of a serpent on his arm, shook the dice and rolled them against the cushion. They kept yelling stuff like "one more time," and "Baby, don't stop now!"

When all the dust had settled, Amanda was jumping up and down and going crazy along with the other folks. She grabbed Luther's arm. "We won, we won!"

Luther was getting embarrassed. "Manda, calm down. It's just two dollars."

"Yeah," Amanda cooed. "But just wait."

So, Luther waited. He waited while Amanda lost the five dollars she'd assigned to the crap table, and she didn't want to play the other games, and would play craps instead. He waited while she decided "that hairy man didn't know what he's doing," and she was glad "he crapped out." He even waited while she was rolling the dice and the crowd was telling her to "let it ride, little lady, let it ride!" Luther just knew she was gonna get bucked off that horse sooner or later.

They didn't have a watch with them because Luther had left it with me, so I'd know what time it was. Luther hadn't thought there wouldn't be a clock anywhere inside. When he realized that there weren't any windows, he said he started feeling closed in. He was getting hungry and needed to use the bathroom. Amanda had a big stack of chips and was still letting it ride, when one of the casino fellas tapped Luther on the shoulder.

"Excuse me, I'm Graves. House Security," he told Luther. "That lady with you?" he said, pointing over to Amanda.

Luther was flustered. "Yes, sir." Luther kept nudging Amanda to get her attention, but she kept waving his hand away. "We got married this afternoon," he told the man.

"Congratulations," he said, shaking Luther's hand. He smelled like cigarettes—everything did—and his hand felt like sandpaper. "Guess you two been celebrating?" he asked, picking up their glasses of root beer and sniffing them. Luther decided he didn't want any more. His eye twitched. The man noticed it. "You all right, son?"

Luther nodded. "I think so. Is there something wrong?"

The man smiled. "Well, that's something we'll need to discuss. Why don't you and your little wife come with me."

Luther thought Amanda had done it. It was bad enough her daddy was going to kill both of them for running off and getting married, but he wasn't going to be too happy having to bail them out of jail. Luther knew he shouldn't have let Amanda talk him into that place. Oh, Lord, thought Luther, this was a whole lot worse than indecent exposure!

Graves was talking on the phone. When the man pushed the dice back at Amanda, Luther grabbed her hands before she could get them.

"Luther, what *are* you doing?" she said.

He picked up her chips and put them in her purse. "C'mon, Manda, I think we in trouble," he said, nodding over to the man on the phone.

"What?" Amanda asked, and her eyes got wide as she looked at the man Luther was pointing to.

They followed Graves upstairs. Amanda clutched her purse. "They're just mad because I was on a winning streak," she whispered to Luther.

"Manda, hush," Luther whispered back.

"But if they ask you, say you're twenty-one," Amanda told him.

Luther stopped dead in his tracks. "Amanda Beaumont," he almost shouted.

Amanda pulled him. "It's Amanda Beaumont Rawlings, thank you. Now c'mon, Luther, and don't be so loud."

Luther was sure they were in trouble now. His hands were sweating by the time they got into the office. It looked more like a living room than an office. There was a room full of wood-grained mohair sofa and chairs. The blood-red carpet matched the drapes. Luther always said red was the color of danger.

The man behind the large wood-grain desk introduced himself as the manager. He wore a gray suit and had one of those "toasted" Lucky Strikes hanging from his pink lips. He looked young, but his hair had gone to salt and pepper. He was hoarse when he talked.

"I heard you two just got married," he said.

Luther nodded. Amanda was quiet.

The man smiled. "I'm not one to pry—really I'm not—but you mind if I ask how old you two are?"

Luther and Amanda both looked at each other. Luther had visions of ending up sharing a cell in jail with someone like the heavy-set man at the dice table with smelly breath and rotten teeth, who was sure to beat the daylights out of Luther because he didn't like him. Then Luther thought about the stories he'd read. What if he did like him—a whole lot? Luther shuddered. Then he decided to leave it in God's hands. He figured he'd messed things up trying to fix it himself. Luther sent Amanda a "please don't go to hell by telling another lie" look.

Amanda poked him in the rib when the man cleared his throat. "Did you hear him, Luther? How old are we?"

Luther stared at her. "How come you asking me? You know how old we are, just like me."

"But he asked *you*," Amanda insisted, trying to smile at the man.

"No he didn't," Luther shot back. "He asked whoever wants to tell him."

Amanda grit her teeth and closed her eyes. "Well, just maybe I don't want to tell him."

"Maybe I don't want to tell him neither," Luther said, and noticed the manager smiling at them.

"Can I see your driver's license?" Graves said, impatiently. Luther took out his wallet and handed his license to Graves. "I'm nineteen and she's seventeen," Luther confessed. Amanda huffed and stamped her feet. She turned her back to Luther.

Graves examined it, nodded, and then handed it to the manager. The manager studied the license. He was strangely quiet. Luther reckoned Graves was trying to remember if he saw him on the wall at the Post Office with the other pictures of wanted criminals—dead or alive. Luther held his breath, waiting for the verdict. He tried to avoid the manager's eyes and stared down at the gold plated name plate on his desk. Bernie VanHorn. I was the only one besides Jake who knew what the "B" in Luther's name stood for. Luther said "Bernard" was bad enough. But he sure wouldn't take kindly to folks calling him Bernie. And here this man was brave enough to put it in gold letters on his desk for the world to see.

Mr. VanHorn ran his fingers through his salt and pepper hair. "Your parents know you here," he said, still studying Luther.

Luther looked toward the ground. "No, sir . . . we . . . eloped."

The man nodded and looked over at Amanda. "Your parents are probably worried about you."

Luther and Amanda looked at each other. "But they'll be happy for us when we get back," Amanda insisted. Sounded like she was trying to convince herself.

The man put out the cigarette butt and took another one out of the gold cigarette case sitting on his desk. "So why elope?" he asked.

"Well, papa's not too pleased right now, but he'll get used to it," Amanda told him. Luther said he didn't look up.

Mr. VanHorn rubbed Luther's picture and looked at it one last time. "And what about your parents?" he said, handing the license back to Luther.

"They're not living anymore," Luther said. "Died close to seven years ago."

Amanda pursed her lips. "His mama did, that is," she pointed out. "Luther still doesn't know where his good-for-nothing—"

"Manda!" Luther shouted. He was huffing by then. "You don't *have* to be telling folks my business!"

Amanda was flustered. "I—I'm sorry, Luther." She took his hand, and Luther calmed down.

"You're from Coolidge. That right?" Mr. VanHorn asked them. They both nodded.

VanHorn cleared his throat and sat on the desk. "You have to be twenty-one to gamble. I'm sure you didn't know that," he said.

Luther felt it was time to speak up. "I'm sorry, Mr. VanHorn. Really I am. I didn't know. I usually don't even gamble—it wasn't fun—all the noise and—I didn't enjoy myself at all."

Amanda elbowed him in the side. "Luther, I think he gets the message," she said through her teeth.

"Well, you do realize I cannot allow you to gamble anymore," Mr. VanHorn told them.

They both nodded.

"But let's do this." He picked up a pad and scratched something a few words on it. "I feel something special inside for you two. You can keep your winnings." He looked over at Graves. "Call it . . . a wedding present." He handed the slip of paper to Graves who raised his eyebrows when he looked at it. Graves turned and went out the door.

Luther and Amanda grabbed each other's hand. "Did you hear that, Luther?" Amanda tried to whisper.

Mr. VanHorn just sat leaning back in his chair, taking a puff now and then on his Lucky. Both Luther and Amanda were quiet, but Amanda could hardly contain herself. Graves was only gone for a few minutes, but to Luther and Amanda it seemed like forever. He came back with a big envelope, and handed it to Mr. VanHorn. Mr. VanHorn glanced through the envelope. He licked and sealed it. Then he turned to Amanda.

"Here," he said, with a smile. "Stick this in your purse so you don't lose it on the way."

Amanda quickly grabbed the envelope and stuffed it out of sight. Luther nodded and stood up. He grabbed Mr. VanHorn's hand and shook it fiercely. "Thank you, thank you," was all he could say.

As they were leaving, Mr. VanHorn called to Luther. "Bernard!" The sound rattled Luther like it did when his mama would call him by his middle name. Quickly he spun around. Luther noticed a sadness in Mr. VanHorn's voice—almost like an apology. Like he understood why Luther's middle name was Bernard. "I've loved a lot of women in my life—some I left—some left me." He sighed. "Anyway, just take care of your wife and treat her right. She deserves it. And I wish you the best," he said, closing the door.

Luther decided to pray for him for being so nice to them. He was glad Mr. VanHorn had wished them the best. He was sure they would need it when they got home. They had escaped the frying pan, but he knew when they got back—it was into the fire for sure.

Chapter Four

Mr. Beaumont ranted and raved, for what seemed to Luther like weeks. When he finished carrying on, he stopped speaking to Luther and Amanda altogether. Amanda's heart was broken. Mr. Beaumont found out I had driven them to Las Vegas, but I didn't worry about him not speaking to me. He never did anyway, even before that—not even when he came in to get one of his horses shoed. But I was glad they had proposed an anti-lynching legislation. Plus, Mr. Beaumont, like everybody else, was too busy worrying about Hitler and the Nazis to concentrate on me too much.

After a few months, he and his wife moved back to Nevada. Luther saw Mrs. Beaumont quite a bit at first, but then even her visits got less and less.

Jake Phillips gave Luther and Amanda a real good deal on a house a few miles from town. It was an old brick house, nice and sturdy. It had a huge back yard—big enough for plenty of kids to play in. Luther and Amanda both wanted a house full of them. Luther pieced off a section to grow tomatoes. He let Amanda have the other side for a rose garden. They never did bloom. The house had three big bedrooms and two bathrooms: one full bathroom with a bathtub, and the other with only a commode and a sink. There was also a roomy cellar and a garage where Luther stored a lot of supplies.

Amanda fixed their house up real nice. She liked bright colors, and decorated everything in the style of the Old West, just like

Luther wanted it. They got along well most of the time, except when it came to where to put family pictures. Luther wasn't too big on putting pictures up. In fact, he didn't like having them taken. "I know what I look like," he used to always say. I was going to draw pictures of both them as a house-warming present, but I bought them some monogrammed towels instead.

Amanda put pictures on the china cabinet, on the walls, on the dumbwaiter, on the tables in the hall—even in the bathrooms.

"Manda," Luther told her, "Everywhere I turn, I got your daddy's face staring at me."

"It makes a house seem more like home," Amanda told him. "And it's my home, not theirs, Luther." Amanda would start cleaning whenever she got nervous. She picked up the broom and pointed it at Luther. "Well, what's wrong with the pictures?"

Luther snatched up the newspaper. "Nothing. But how come we gotta have so many? It's not that I don't like your folks, but I don't allow nobody except you in the bathroom or the bedroom with me. I sure don't take kindly to having other faces leering at me."

"Okay," Amanda said. "But the rest of them have to stay. All right?"

Luther nodded, pleased that he'd won his first argument.

To Luther, going to church was like brushing his teeth. It wasn't something he thought much about. It was something he did every Sunday.

"C'mon, wake up," he called to Amanda, shaking her after he heard George and Delores Paines' rooster crowing at the top of his lungs. "We gotta eat breakfast before we leave."

Amanda yawned, blinking her eyes from the sun starting to peer in through the flowered curtains. "What time is it?"

"Almost seven-thirty."

"Seven-thirty? There's no way we'll make eight o'clock mass," Amanda told him, turning over to go back to sleep.

"Mass?" Luther said. "Manda, we not going to mass. Services start at nine."

Amanda pursed her lips and ran her fingers through her hair. "Luther, you know I was born and raised Catholic."

"Yeah," Luther said, going to the closet and laying out his brown Sunday-go-to-meeting suit.

Amanda stared at him. "Why, all the Beaumont family are Catholics."

"Yeah," Luther said again, not looking at her. He took his brown loafers out of the shoe box.

"And they have a nice big one up in Flagstaff."

"Uh-huh. You seen my belt to my pants?"

"Hanging on the door," Amanda told him. "Luther, it has the most beautiful glass-stained windows. The first thing you hear when you drive up is Mrs. Doyle making sweet music on the brand new Steinway papa donated a few years ago."

"Mmm-hmph," said Luther, washing his face.

"It's so spiritual. Just sweeps you off your feet."

Luther came in and pointed to the clock. "I'm getting ready to take my shower," he said. "You've talked for almost fifteen minutes, now. I'll be leaving out of here at eight-thirty. We can talk more about the church you used to go to on the way."

With that, he went into the bathroom. Amanda sat there dumbfounded. She probably pouted for another five minutes, but when she realized Luther was intentionally ignoring her, she hurried up and got ready for church. She looked pleased that Luther had breakfast waiting for her, but she complained all the way to church. She complained after they got there. She said the church was old and shabby-looking. She said the sign with Reverend Hayes' name and church name on it wasn't fancy enough. She complained about the wooden steps and the white paint that was chipping on the side of the building.

Amazingly though, she was quiet all during the service. I figured she was probably too busy trying to listen in on my mama and Mabel's latest gossip session. We were sitting right in front of Luther and Amanda. Reverend Hayes had started losing members to Reverend Ward's church. Finally, Reverend Hayes said it was "time Coolidge took a stand against segregation," especially since he needed the black folks' tithes and offerings.

It turned out that Amanda was quiet in public whenever Delores Paine was around. Delores had a love for tiny hats, and she had on one shaped like a sail boat propped to the side of her large head of black curls. Her curls were a strong contrast to her ivory white skin. Kind of reminded me of piano keys. And Delores always smelled like lemons. She had had come in with her husband and deliberately sat next to Amanda and Luther.

"'Morning," George said, rubbing his balding scalp. He sat his derby in his lap, and Luther could tell his dark brown eyes were apologizing to him for the incident a few days after Luther and Amanda moved in.

Luther said he was outside bamming on the porch. Some of the boards were loose and he'd been fixing them. He could smell Delores before she came through the fence.

"Hello," she cooed, sashaying up the walk. She was carrying something wrapped in a paper bag.

"Howdy," Luther answered back.

Delores gave out a phony laugh. It sounded like a rusty hinge needing some oil. "I'm Delores Paine, just across the way. Here," she said, handing the bag to Luther. "I know you just moved in a few days ago. And since I know most men don't cook—well, it's an apple cobbler—for desert."

"Thank you," Luther said, and set it down on the ground. Delores looked flustered. "Well, I just wondered if there's anything I can help you with?"

Luther heard the screen door slam. Amanda stood there with the cold glass of water he'd asked for ten minutes ago. She'd called to him that she was "too busy" right then. Luther smiled and pointed to Amanda. "I think I got all the help I can use," he said, reaching for the glass. Amanda just stood there glaring at Delores.

Delores' square face turned red. "Oh, hello," she said.

"Hello," Amanda said, smiling through clenched teeth. "Thank you for the desert. I'm sorry you can't stay."

Delores grabbed the bag and switched back in a huff back down to her house.

"Manda, that wasn't neighborly. You know that." Luther took the glass from her.

"Of all the nerve," Amanda said, still watching Delores.

He put down the hammer. "Seems you found time to bring me some water after Delores got here."

Amanda glared at him. "And she's a married woman, at that!"

"Wonder what she was planning on helping me with," Luther said, grinning up at her.

"Oh you hush up! Dinner will be ready in ten minutes."

He confessed to me he kept grinning as he heard the screen door slam.

So there was Delores, sitting next to Amanda in church, with her arm wrapped through George's. She had a smug look on her face. After all, what could she possibly want with Luther? She was married to the school superintendent. Just as Eddie Hickerwood, the Sheriff's son, finished the Bible reading, a tall, light-skinned black man and his wife walked in. Of course all eyes was on them because nobody had seen them before. His wife was very attractive. Her skin was a dark peach-color and she had high cheekbones and pretty green eyes. I figured they were just visiting.

It was the last Sunday of the month and the children's choir was on the program. It was a big choir, most of them the Taylors' kids. Vanessa Stewart was only fourteen years old, but she had a beautiful voice. She would rock the whole house up at Lola Faye's Cafe in Randolph. Everybody knew she was the best singer in the choir, but Reverend Hayes' oldest daughter, Charlene, always sang lead in church. She was blurting out "This Little Light of Mine," while we were all wishing she would shine hers somewhere else. Reverend Hayes was tapping his foot to keep time, and his wife Constance was at the organ nodding like it was the most beautiful thing they'd ever heard. Their youngest daughter, Tammy, who was five years old, was holding onto the sides of her dress and rocking back and forth.

As usual, when Reverend Hayes started his sermon, my mama Lucille and Aunt Mabel started theirs.

Mama leaned over to Mabel. "Did you hear about the Taylors?"

Mabel shook her head. "Uh-uh. What's that?"

"Here tell they done had another one," Mama said.

"Not another one, Lue?"

"As I live and breathe. Now, Mabel, you know seventeen young 'uns is way too many."

"I know that's right."

My mama was quiet while the ushers—Bert, Sam, Doc and Ramon—Doc Peterson's son, passed the collection basket. Mama put in her ten percent in the basket, and then put in her last two cents in the gossip.

"Course Ardel named him Danny after her husband." Then Mama reared back and looked at Mabel out the corner of her eye. "That lil' baby chile just as yellow as he wanna be—and every one of the Taylors blacker than you and me, Mabel, put together!"

After services, it was segregation time again. The white folks congregated together inside, and the black folks congregated together outside. The white folks were headed for the church social later that evening, and the black folks were headed for the fish fry at the Taylors'. Now, the white folks were invited to the fish fry, and the black folks were invited to the church social, but we all knew who was gonna be at what. A few "hello's," some "howdy's" and "how are you's," and about a dozen "chile, how you been's," and folks started meandering to their cars and trucks.

Luther opened the truck for Amanda to get in. I waved to her and she waved back. Luther saw me rubbing my knuckles. "I'll be right back," Luther told her. "I need to talk to Hawk." He ambled over to me.

Just then, my mama brought the light-skinned man and his pretty green-eyed wife over to us. "And this is Hawk, my son," my mama Lucille said, with a smile. "This is Mr. Rawlings." Then she pointed to the man and his wife. "This is Mr. and Mrs. Simmons. He's a lawyer," she said, proudly.

Mr. Simmons grinned and his wife looked a bit embarrassed, but she smiled and nodded. I noticed he kept twirling a piece of wadded paper in his hand. Seems he had a nervous habit of doing that a lot, I learned later.

He reached for my hand with his free hand. "I'm Earl Simmons," he said. He took two cards out of his inside vest and handed one to me and one to Luther. "Attorney-at-Law," he added.

Now we never seen many black lawyers round this part before. To tell the truth, I never even seen *one* before. Mr. Simmons put his hand around his wife. "This is my wife, Rachel."

I nodded. She was the most beautiful woman I'd ever seen. Luther shook his hand. "Nice to meet you, Mr. Simmons. I'm Luther." Luther pointed to Amanda who was sitting in the truck muttering to herself. "That's my wife over there—Amanda."

"Yes, it's good to meet you." Mr. Simmons tipped his hat to Amanda. She nodded and smiled. "I hear congratulations are in order, Luther. Lucille tells me your wife is expecting." My mama made sure to bring newcomers up to date on everything.

"We have a nineteen-year-old. Alura. She's away at college right now," Mrs. Simmons said. Her voice was soft and sweet.

Luther nodded and looked over at Amanda who looked depressed.

"Now, I know you two joining us for the fish fry?" my mama asked them.

Mr. Simmons looked at his wife. "Sure," she said, with a smile, pulling her shawl up on her small shoulders.

My mama walked them over to their car, still talking. Luther noticed me still rubbing my knuckles. "You going to the church social this evening?" he asked me.

I shook my head. "No, after the fish fry I'm driving my mama and Aunt Mabel over to the bus station to pick up Aunt Mabel's ex-husband's niece, Olivia. Wants to be a nurse up at Florence. She's coming here to live, I guess."

"That why you so nervous?" Luther asked.

I stopped rubbing my knuckles and shook my head.

"Don't have to tell me if you don't want to," Luther said. "I just wondered what was wrong, that's all."

I saw my mama looking my way, so I lowered my voice. "Remember that girl you saw me with last summer?"

Luther nodded. "Who could forget? Her melons was bigger than the ones I bought at Shopes."

I snickered in spite of how I was feeling. "Well, now she got another big melon." I made a big circle around my belly.

Luther's eyes got big and he turned red. He rubbed the back of his neck. "Don't rightly know what to say, Hawk. Your mama know?"

"She will this evening. Can't keep nothing from Mama Lucille for too long, you know that. Baby's due in two months."

Luther wrinkled his lips and looked over at Amanda.

I tugged at my tie. "Least yaw'll had the sense to get married first," I said.

"Well, things happen," Luther said. Then he gave me a pat on the shoulder. "Let's go up to Coolidge Dam next Friday. Give your mind a vacation for a while."

I smiled at him. "Bet you do that all the time, huh, Luther—give your mind a vacation."

"Yeah," Luther said, and then he grinned and pointed his Bible at me. "God gonna get you for that, Hawk."

It was starting to drizzle. My mama decided she was through talking for a while and yelled over to me. "Hawk, c'mon."

I sighed. "All right," I told Luther. "After today, I might *need* some place to go."

"Well, we got an extra room until the baby comes, if you need it." Luther tucked his Bible under his arm. "Just remember, children are a blessing from God—no matter how they get here."

On their way home, Amanda picked up her complaining where she'd left off. "And those are the hardest seats I've ever seen. Don't they believe in turning on the cooler?"

Luther looked straight ahead. "Manda, it's wintertime."

"Still, it's so stuffy in that little place. And don't they have a choir? My Lord! The way that girl ruined that song *Nearer My God To Thee,* it's a wonder God will let her within ten miles of him."

Luther couldn't help but laugh. "Now, Manda, she wasn't that bad."

But Amanda was on a roll. "Oh, and that Reverend Hayes. I've never in my life seen a man with nothing to say take so long saying it!"

Luther pulled up into their yard. He took Amanda's gloved hand. "I'm sorry you didn't enjoy services, honey. Tell you what— just to be fair—we can go to your church up in Flagstaff next time."

Amanda gave him a look. "Not on your life, Luther Rawlings. You just keep on taking me to that church. I've got to get on the committee and start fixing things!"

Luther smiled and shook his head. He was sure he was never going to understand womenfolk.

It seems George Paine had invited a few folks from the school board to the church social at Reverend Hayes' home. Even Jim Winters, the principal of Coolidge High was there. He never showed up at church, but he was always there for the after-church festivities.

Luther wasn't too happy that it turned more into a meeting than a social gathering. They had all congregated inside Reverend Hayes' living room. The place was filled with smelling cigars and pipes, and Sheriff Hickerwood was propped up on the sofa chewing tobacco. Luther knew Jake Phillips wouldn't be there. No matter how many times Luther would invite him to something, Jake said if he didn't come to church, he wasn't about to come to the "after-church."

Luther got tired of hearing about how something had to "be done about unions," and how unions was "giving all the jobs to the colored folks and foreigners." He walked through the hallway to check on Amanda in the parlor with the other womenfolk. Sam had come up to him and was bending his ear about how the "the Nazis was bad enough—now it's those doggone Japs!"

Luther was half-listening. Amanda was in a room with womenfolk almost twice her age. Delores Paine was dominating the conversation about her ex-husband who became an alcoholic after his mild heart attack and had to give up his lumber business. Luther told me later that it was no small wonder that Delores Paine's first husband was an alcoholic, because she could drive anybody to drink.

Amanda was sitting there nibbling on a piece of cheese and olive. She saw Luther looking over at her. She made funny faces at him and mimicked Delores when she thought nobody was looking. Luther laughed, just as Sam was saying how hard they were making it for him to keep his liquor license. Luther turned to him. "Sorry," he said, and Sam went back into the meeting.

Beulah Peterson, Doc's wife, pushed her bifocals up on her nose. She caught Amanda mimicking Delores. Amanda's eyes grew wide with embarrassment. Beulah smiled. "Uh, that's nice, Delores," Beulah said, waving Delores to be quiet. "I want to hear from Amanda. Dear child, my husband tells me you and Luther are expecting."

Delores sniffed and reached for her tea. "Oh . . . well, I . . ."

Amanda saw all eyes turn on her, and she smiled. "Doc says in five months."

Beulah saw Luther watching them. She nodded. "I hope married life isn't too stressful."

Amanda followed her line of sight to Luther. "Oh, it's just fine. Luther is so sweet. He's working real hard for Jake. He's cutting hair now. I'm very proud of him, and he can fix just about anything you can imagine. Why just the other day—"

"Seems to me if he was all that good of a husband, he'd buy you a house in better shape that didn't need so much fixing up," Delores spat out.

Amanda didn't say anything. She just picked up her tea and took a sip. Luther's eye twitched, thinking that Amanda was acting too calm.

Delores tossed her head of black curls. "In fact, now that I think about it, I believe it was that house that last month kept us from winning the City of the Sun's Best Homes and Gardens award."

Amanda glared at her. Beulah patted Amanda's arm. "Don't worry, dear, I'm sure that little garden of yours will have fine roses one day," Beulah told her.

"I guess she is doing the best she can," Delores added. Then she flared out her white ruffled dress. It looked brand new. "As I was saying earlier, George is so thoughtful. Sometimes I have to just ask him to stop buying me things."

Amanda was gritting her teeth. Luther's eye was still twitching. He made a move to go into the parlor, but Bert grabbed his arm. "Hey, Luther, you see the fight the other day?"

"Fight?" Luther was still watching Amanda.

"Graciano was something else."

Luther nodded. But he knew Rocky was nothing compared to Amanda when she got riled up. He kept his eyes peeled on Amanda and Delores. If only Delores would shut up. But he might as well been wishing that taxes was something the government paid us.

Delores went to twirling her pearl necklace. "Oh, we had the most beautiful wedding ceremony in Scottsdale. All of me and George's family were there." She flashed her hundred-and-one teeth at Amanda. "Why, it just wouldn't have been proper just to run off and get married. Seems like young folks these days do that a lot. But a lady would never think of doing such a—"

Luther tried his best to get over to Amanda, but he was a step too late. Delores was wearing every drop of Amanda's tea. Her face and the front of her new dress were soaked. One of her false eyelashes looked like a caterpillar on her face, and her mouth hung open in disbelief. Luther said that the other women, including Beulah, were trying their best to stifle their laughter. Delores stared down at her new dress. Luther grabbed Amanda's arm in one hand and had his hat in the other. Time to go.

"Thank you all for inviting us," Luther said, pulling Amanda out the door. "But we have to get up early tomorrow."

Delores picked up the bottom of her skirt and run into the back room. Luther thought Amanda would be talking about her victory on the way home, but she was quiet. By the time Luther drove up into the yard, she was in tears.

"Oh, Luther, I'm sorry. I don't know why I did that," she said, sobbing.

Luther turned off the engine. "I do, Manda."

She sniffed. "You do?"

"Yeah, because deep down you know Delores is right." He wiped her tears with his handkerchief.

"What do you mean?"

"You know, about me not being able to give you a proper wedding."

Amanda wiped her eyes and sat up straight. "Now, Luther, you stop that. Delores Paine is a snob! Why anybody knows it's not how or where you get married. It's what you do with your marriage. Courting somebody is easy. And anybody can put on a big ceremony. But it's whether or not you still together for the next forty or fifty years—that's what matters!"

Luther shook his head and hugged her. "Amanda Faye Rawlings, sometimes you amaze me."

She kissed him. "I know, Luther."

When they got out of the truck, Luther started to giggle. "What?" Amanda asked, started to giggle too. "What's so funny?"

"I was . . . I was just picturing Delores standing there like a wet chicken," he said. "Now that's the first time I seen her with her mouth wide open and wasn't no words coming out." He laughed. "Don't believe you did that, Manda."

"Well, it was getting hot in that room. I was just helping Delores cool off, that's all," she said, laughing with him.

"I think you might've done just the opposite," Luther told her.

Amanda giggled. Then she turned to Luther as he opened up the front door. "There's only one problem."

"What's that?" Luther asked.

"Guess who's President of the Women's Committee?"

"Not Delores Paine?"

"I'm afraid so."

It's a good thing Amanda didn't get on the Women's Committee. It was getting close to her term to deliver, and she was losing weight instead of gaining like Doc Peterson said she was supposed to.

Mrs. Beaumont came to stay with them to take care of Amanda. Luther was spending more time at the shop so he could save up some more money with the baby coming, and to pay for Amanda's doctor bills.

Jake Phillips was especially happy to hear that Amanda was going to have a baby. "Boy, I didn't think you had it in you," he told Luther. "So, what you want—a lil' boy or a lil' gal?"

Luther shrugged. "Don't matter, Jake, as long as it's healthy."

Jake foamed up Sam's face. "Well, better hope it's a boy, 'cause them lil' gals ain't nothing but trouble, running off and getting married behind they daddy's back."

Luther's smile dropped as he picked up the clippers. Jake said it like he knew something about girls running off.

"You never had a girl of your own, Jake," Luther said slowly. "Have you? So don't go telling me about little girls."

Jake must have seen the sadness on Luther's face. "Now, boy, I wasn't talking about you and Amanda, if that's what you're thinking. Aw c'mon—don't go dragging no long face. Congrats. You done good." Jake wiped his hands on his apron. "I guess you best be hurrying up shaving Doc. You gone need to do a hell of a lot more customers to pay for that new young 'un."

Luther's eye twitched as he noticed a short fat man in a black suit sitting in the corner reading one of the magazines. He felt uncomfortable about the man.

Jake rubbed his chin. "I guess we could work out a different take-in split," he said, looking over at Luther. "Guess you know what you doing, now. What you say, boy? Think you worth eighty percent of your take?"

Luther's mouth fell open. He'd been getting fifty-five up until then. "You serious?"

Jake smiled and started shaving Sam.

Luther wanted to hug him. "Thanks, Jake. Thank you!"

The man who'd been sitting in the corner took a watch out of his vest pocket. He looked over at Jake. "I can't wait, Mr. Phillips. I have a two o'clock. I'll be back."

"Yeah, yeah, yeah," Jake said, waving him off.

"Who was that," Luther asked.

"My nemesis," Doc said from his chair.

"Your what?" Luther said.

"He's the new mortician. You know, I heal them—he buries them."

"Mortician," Luther said softly, and he reckoned he could feel a chill run up his spine, and back down again.

Jake smacked his lips. "Yep," he said. "He's from Tucson. Been trying to get me to sell him this place for a funeral parlor. If that ain't the most foolish thing! I told him I ain't a budging. He can have my body when I'm through, but he ain't a touching my shop if I can help it!"

"Once you dead, you won't have much to say about it," Sam told him.

Jake shook a fist at him. "Yeah, that's what you think, you cock-eyed yella-bellied—" Jake cut his words short and glanced over at Luther. "So, is Amanda feeling any better?"

"She's doing okay. Right, Doc?" Luther asked.

Doc Peterson was holding his head stiffly. He didn't want Luther to cut off too much like last time. "I told her to take it easy. Just make sure she takes her pills."

"I'm trying," Luther told him. "But you know Manda, she keeps thinking the pills will hurt the baby."

Doc sighed. "To be honest, Luther, they're not the best for the child. But I'm more concerned with Amanda's health right now."

Luther said he felt something well up inside him. "But she is going to be all right?"

Doc didn't say anything.

"Of course she is boy," Jake said.

Luther finished cutting Doc's hair and then gave him a shave. Doc rubbed his wrinkled face. "Mighty smooth, Luther." Doc looked over at Jake as he took out his wallet. "I'm glad you gave him a raise. He deserves it."

When both Sam and Doc were gone, Jake put up his feet and lit up a stogie. "So, boy, yaw'll picked out a name yet?"

Luther tried to contain himself. "If it's a girl, Amanda says we'll call her Luthella Bernice."

Jake scrunched up his face. "Luthella, huh?"

Luther nodded.

Jake shook his head. "And if it's a boy?"

Luther's chest swelled. "Luther Bernard Rawlings, the Second!"

Jake blew out a smoke ring. "The Second? Hell, one of yaw'll is bad enough. The world's not ready for two of yaw'll!"

Jake was right. The baby never cried. Never made a sound. Amanda just wouldn't stop bleeding. She didn't look like herself laying in that casket. Luther wasn't ready for the tiny casket next to Amanda's. Mr. Beaumont cussed Luther something awful. Called him every name he could think of. Said he should never have let Luther around Amanda in the first place. Even Mrs. Beaumont couldn't bring herself to face Luther. Not a one of them even considered how Luther was feeling.

Luther couldn't bear to say goodbye to Amanda. In fact, he was determined not to say goodbye. He left before they put her body in the ground. He didn't go back to work right away. He managed to get by off his savings and Amanda's insurance money. He worked in Amanda's garden. He tried to take his mind off her, but everything reminded him of Amanda. Jake was patient. He didn't even hassle Luther about coming in.

I visited Luther when I got the chance. Luther knew I'd had a boy, Tommy Lee. The girl I got pregnant had wanted to give it up for adoption, so I kept him. My mama Lucille agreed to help me raise him. But, out of respect for Luther and what he'd just gone through, I never talked about Tommy Lee. Luther wanted to talk, and I kept apologizing to him. He told me to stop—that it wasn't my fault—that it wasn't anybody's fault, but his. When I tried to convince him otherwise, he shrugged me off, and said, "It's just God's way."

Luther took a drive up to Coolidge Dam for some fishing. I wanted to go with him, but I knew he needed to be alone. He didn't catch a single fish. He didn't care. He tried to figure out what he'd done so wrong in his life to lose Amanda. It just didn't seem real to him. Every night when he went to sleep he kept expecting her to roll over and say, "Wake up, Luther, you having a bad dream."

Luther didn't go back to work for three months. It was that afternoon, around closing time, that Jake caught him staring off into space.

"You all right, boy?" Jake asked him.

Luther didn't respond.

"You know, it ain't healthy to keep things bottled up inside."

"I'm fine, Jake."

"All right, but you let me know," he said, tapping his bony shoulder. "'Cause I may be close to sixty, but I'm stronger than I look."

Luther hugged him. Then Luther talked and talked. And Jake listened. And then Luther let it all out. He bawled like a baby until all he could do was whimper. Jake never said anything about that day. Never even brought it up when he got mad at Luther. Luther appreciated that.

Chapter Five

We had celebrated being able to watch Frankie D on television. Now he had died, and most of what the New Deal promised, Truman tried to make into a Fair Deal. At least I was getting seventy cents an hour. I couldn't really complain. It was a time of uniting and trying to find a common ground. Churches were organizing and holding councils, the Nazis had finally surrendered, and NATO came into being. Truman had even ordered the military to desegregate.

But most black folks found themselves still not being able to eat at the same lunch counters, ride the same buses, or use the same bathrooms as white folks. Some of the black folks from the east coast who'd moved to Phoenix was talking about Apartheid and Nelson Mandela, and the racism that was going on in South Africa. I couldn't sympathize at the time. We were having a hard time just trying to desegregate what used to be called Jake's Place.

Luther said he understood what black folks meant when we said, "We take one step forward, and we get pushed back two." Seems Luther's hopes would be built up one moment, and the next thing he knew, he was back to square one. We were both dealing with hoping and dreaming for something we were never gonna have. Don't know which one of us was worse off. Luther was still pining away for Amanda, and I was pining away for Mrs. Rachel Simmons.

Luther recovered better than I did—at least he seemed to. Jake retired and sold the shop to him. Earl Simmons set up his lawyer's office out of his home. Aside from helping folks, mostly black folks, read and review contracts and settling minor disputes, he talked about running for sheriff. Luther said Chuck Yeager sure could have used Mr. Simmons that summer after Chuck Yeager had broken the sound barrier. Seems Mr. Yeager would have been sued over his airplane. Luther said people would sue you over anything they could think of.

I got out of the blacksmithing business and made all right money fixing up cars. It wasn't too hard making the transition. It was still "horsepower" any way you look at it. Danny Taylor Sr. had trained me real good and then sold the garage to me. It was now Hawk's Garage, and my mama was awfully proud to have a real business owner in the family. She never talked about Willie Jackson. In fact, nobody talked about him. Tommy Lee was nine years old and always ready and willing to help me. He learned the names of tools and brought them to me whenever I asked. He had my height and bone structure, and looked like he was already sixteen years old. Luther had been bugging me about coming in to get a haircut and a shave. He said it was his shop and he didn't care what nobody else said. I decided to take him up on his offer.

I was kind of slow that day—only had two cars to work on. Luther didn't know I was coming. I almost changed my mind when I saw Jake Phillips sitting inside. I guess he felt he had to keep an eye on his old place, and he'd come in to help from time to time. Bert and Sam were playing checkers in the corner. Bert's wife was always filling in for Bert at the Trading Post while he was supposed to be running errands. But, as usual, he was at Jake's Place trying to beat Sam at checkers. I held my breath and went in. I saw Luther's right eye twitch soon as he saw me. But he smiled anyway.

"Hawk," Luther said. "C'mon in. I'm glad you came."

I saw Bert and Sam pretending not to see me. A thin man in cowboy boots and hat grunted and turned up his nose when he saw me, like he was suddenly aware of a foul smell. He glared at Luther, grabbed his hat, and left like I was contagious or something. Jake's green eyes had a wickedness about them. He took out his fat stogie and pursed his lips. His eyes followed me real steady as I went over and took a seat on the vinyl sofa. A whole minute went by before Jake broke into one of his threatening drawls.

"Since when you start letting darkies get they hair cut in here, Luther?"

I tried to remain calm, but I could feel the veins starting to pop in my forehead.

Jake flashed his tobacco-stained smile. "I heard darkies is like a barrel full of crabs. You know, soon as one of 'em is lucky to start crawling to the top, the others jumps up and pulls him right back down!"

Jake blew smoke rings in my direction. Luther didn't say a word, but I knew he was watching me to see what I was gonna do. The tension was so thick you could slice it in pieces—and still have some left over. I started easing my hand inside the grease-stained pocket of my overalls for my knife. I was trying to scare Jake, but he kept pressing his luck.

"Maybe that's why none of 'em ever amount to nothing," he said, "excepting maybe grease monkeys!"

That was the last straw. I stood up then—all six-four, two-eighty pounds of me. My blood was boiling. I could take everything else from Jake—everything except being a called a monkey—not by him. Luther said my nostrils were flaring and he could see smoke coming out of them. He knew I carried about that big snake knife, and he was sure there was gonna be trouble. Bert and Sam, those old chickens, started easing toward the door.

I came over and stood in front of Jake. Had never been that close to him before. He was so short, and so thin, and so old. I almost felt sorry for him.

"Now c'mon, Hawk," Luther said to me, "Jake is just making a joke—right, Jake?"

Jake didn't say a word. Just kept puffing and grinning like he had a death wish or something. Luther tried to grab my arm. I wouldn't let it budge. I just stood there. Luther could see my chest rising and falling, like I was contemplating what to do with Jake's remains.

"Now, c'mon," Luther pleaded again, "before we all do something I'm gonna regret. You know I can't afford to lose no more customers."

Luther tried to smile, but I knew my silence was deafening to his soul. His hands had started to shake. Jake was sucking his teeth. Luther and I both knew Jake was nervous. Willie Jackson said that's how he knew Jake was bluffing when they played cards—Jake would start to suck his teeth and blow smoke rings in the air. I knew too, though, Jake boasted all the time about the .22 he carried around with him. Luther knew I was all for fighting hand-to-hand, but guns were something they never should have invented, as far as I was concerned. Even my snake knife was only for gutting the bass me and Luther caught.

Luther liked both me and Jake. What was he gonna do? He decided to come stand between me and Jake, facing me. He stared up into my nose. He said it reminded him of a double-barreled shot gun.

"Now look here, Hawk," Luther said, "you ought to know by now that words don't really hurt nobody. And what your mama Lucille gonna say she find out you been fighting? And what kind of model you setting for Tommy Lee?"

Luther didn't know that day how hurt I was. Seemed like he was siding with Jake. I felt like he trusted Jake more than me. I looked right over Luther's head at Jake.

Luther was determined. "So, if you have to fight somebody, it's got to be me."

That burned a whole right in my gut. Luther would be the last person I'd want to fight.

"Course you'd probably beat the daylights out of me," Luther went on. "But I can't have you hurting Jake. I know he's a redneck—but he's much too little and too old for you to be fighting him." Then Luther grinned up at me.

I looked down at him—right into his dark brown eyes. I could see him pleading that I would forget about what Jake had said.

I released the hold on my knife and reached into my pocket. I could hear Sam and Bert gasp behind me. Luther's eye twitched and blinked. He said my silence was about as long as Reverend Hayes' sermons. The difference being everybody was wanting to know what I was gonna say or do next.

They all watched me take out the round ball of tin foil. Luther breathed. I unwrapped the chocolate and stuffed it into my mouth. I smiled as I chewed. Luther shook his head and let out a breath, and his eye stopped twitching.

Jake jabbed one of his bony fingers into Luther's back. "Hey boy, who you calling old?"

I shook my head. I couldn't hold it any longer. Luther said at first a light wrinkle appeared around the corner of my lips. Bert and Sam wiped the sweat off their feathers when they heard me laugh. I laughed so hard I almost choked on my candy.

Jake sat back down. "Well, what you waiting for," he said to Luther. "You got a customer."

Luther smiled and draped the sheet around me as I sat down in the chair.

Jake put out the cigar and rubbed his chin. "Hawk Williams, your daddy would have kicked the living daylights out of me."

"I'm not Willie Jackson," I told him.

Jake nodded. "So you ain't. But you probably hate my guts, don't you?"

I looked at the ground. The only person I ever hated was Willie Jackson. Couldn't hate him no more. He was gone.

"Yeah," Jake went on. "You think I had something to do with your daddy's death?"

I was still quiet.

"Your daddy tell you about me?"

I looked at Jake. I knew he could see it in my eyes. He stared at me for a moment and nodded his head. He looked over and saw Bert and Sam with their mouths hung open. "What yaw'll staring at, you bug-eyed pole cats?"

They quickly went back to their checker game. Then Jake got up and stretched. "I've got to go. See yaw'll later," he said, and then waddled out the door.

Luther and me both smiled at each other through the mirror. Luther called Jake later that evening to thank him for what he'd done.

"Ain't nothing to thank me for. I'm probably going soft in my old age."

"I'm glad," Luther told him.

"Well, get off this phone so I can go have a drink. I got a date with Velma."

Luther laughed. "Velma? When you getting married to the Court Clerk, Jake?"

"Now don't be putting no curses on me, boy. Marriage ain't for everybody."

"See you later, Jake."

"Yeah."

If Jake happened to be there whenever I came in, he still gave me a hard time, but there was no tension. I think he did it because it was expected of him. I just put up with him.

Luther had helped me with Jake, but he said there was nothing he could do about my feelings for Mrs. Simmons. And he warned me not to do anything about it. My head knew what was right, but the rest of me didn't care what my head thought about it. As a lawyer, Mr. Simmons was out of town a lot. He talked more to Luther than he did to me. Luther said Mr. Simmons was so proud of his daughter, Alura. He said Alura refused to live in Coolidge. He said she was born in New Orleans, and that's where she wanted to live. He helped her get an apartment after she graduated from college. She had a job teaching at the Institute for the Blind. She double majored in Communication and Special Education.

"She's even studying sign language," Mrs. Simmons told me one day when she brought her car in for me to take a look at her brakes. She said the brakes were making some kind of "eeeeee" sound. I smiled because one of her cute little nostrils flared and her teeth sparkled when she talked. I told her she should leave the car with me so I could check out the brakes later. I offered to give her a ride back to her house.

"Why, thank you, Hawk," she said. She liked me too. I could tell. But as luck would have it, who would show up—Luther. I looked at Mrs. Simmons and she started fidgeting with her hat and turning a little red.

I tried to get rid of Luther by telling him that Mrs. Simmons was having trouble with her car, and I was going to have to drive her home. Luther just had a stupid grin on his face all the while I was talking.

"Think I'll have to leave my truck here, Hawk," Luther said, nodding his meddlesome old head. "I can ride with you to drop off Mrs. Simmons, and then you can drop me off at the barber shop."

I knew what Luther was doing. It was right, but I still didn't like it. "I guess so," I told him.

Mrs. Simmons was quiet the whole time. Luther, sitting conveniently between us in Mrs. Simmon's car, talked about every married couple he could think of in town. Never once mentioned him and Amanda. It didn't surprise me though.

"How long you and Mr. Simmons been married?" Luther asked her.

I think the question surprised her. "Oh . . . well, it's twenty-five years next December."

Luther smiled and nudged me in the side. "Wow, twenty-five years! Sure is nice, don't you think so, Hawk?

"Yeah," I said, grinding my teeth through my smile. "That's real nice."

"He's due back in a day or two, ain't he?" Luther asked.

"Yes, that's right, he is," she said quietly.

"Well, tell him I said to come on in and have a haircut when he gets back," Luther called to her, when I dropped her off.

"Yes . . . I'll do that." She almost let her handbag fall. She looked over at me. "Thank you for dropping me off, Hawk. I really appreciate it. I'll . . . I'll send Earl over to collect the car." With that, she picked up her skirt and couldn't get in the house fast enough.

Luther had the stupidest smile on his face. "What?" I growled at him.

"For *everything?*" Luther said.

"Get your mind out of the gutter. She brought her car over because her brakes were making some funny noises, like I said."

"Uh huh. And wasn't yesterday the engine making a coughing noise?"

I tried to tune him out.

"And on Wednesday the wheels was wheezing?"

"All right, but I was just gonna give her a ride home. That's all."

Luther rubbed his chin. "Um hmm. Well, tell you what. I got a special today on haircuts. Look like you could use one. Give you one free of charge."

That made me do a double-take. "You ain't never give nobody a free nothing. Most you ever do is half-price."

Luther smiled. "Well, I feel kind of sorry for you."

"Oh really? Why is that?"

Luther shrugged his shoulders. "Well, seeing as you might have to be about running for your life, soon as Mr. Simmons find out you sweet on his woman."

I slammed on the brakes just in front of the barber shop. "Now Luther . . . we friends now . . . I know you ain't . . ."

"Course not. I won't have to. You gone tell him by the way you keep looking at Mrs. Simmons."

"It shows that much?"

"Sticks out like you in a snow storm." Luther started giggling.

"That ain't funny," I told him.

"Aw c'mon. Treat you to a soda pop."

We went inside. Bert and Sam were playing checkers over in the corner. Sam was cheating as usual. Jake was sitting in one of the barber chairs with his short little legs propped up on one of the arms.

"Where in the Sam Hill you been, boy?"

"Huh?" Sam said, looking up.

"I ain't talking to you, you lazy one-eyed goat," Jake drawled. "I 'spose you done forgot you got customers today?"

"Sorry, Jake," Luther said, going over and bringing out a bottle of root beer and a bottle of strawberry. He handed me the strawberry. "Me and Hawk had some business."

"You and Hawk had some . . . what?!"

I sat in the other barber chair and stared down at Jake.

"Hmph," Jake spat out. "You sposed to be taking care of your shop business." Then he settled "Well, c'mon boy, I need a haircut, and I'm aging by the minute."

Luther washed his hands and draped the apron around Jake's bony shoulders. Sam moved his toothpick to one side and winked over at Bert. "Okay, Jake, here's one for you," he said.

"I'm listening."

"When Hank Aaron—"

"You listening, boy?" Jake said to Luther.

Luther nodded.

"Can I finish?" Sam said.

"Well, c'mon you mangy dog, I ain't got all day."

"As I was saying, when Hank Aaron was in the National League, did he ever, and I mean ever, hit a home run against *Cleveland* in a regular season game?" Sam's neck jumped when he said the word Cleveland. Bert was snickering, and a hole appeared where his front tooth used to be. Luther figured something had to be up.

Jake grinned smugly. "Cleveland? Hell, you gone have to come up with something better than that! Everybody who's got a lick of sense know full well—"

Luther tapped Jake on the shoulder. "Wait a minute, Jake."

"Boy, I know you good at this. But I knows the answer this time."

"I'm not saying you don't—well—how much you got bet this time?"

"Same as usual—five Georgie-Porgies."

Sam's smug look matched Jake's. "Care to double it this time?" he said. His ears spaced further apart when he grinned.

Jake took out his stogie. "Hell, it's your money."

"When you right, you right." Sam nudged Bert in his ribs who was dying to bust out laughing.

Luther whispered in Jake's ear. He looked puzzled up at him. "You sure, boy?"

Luther nodded.

"All right," Jake said. "Go for what you know."

"The answer is *yes*," Luther said, striking a pose like Perry Mason. "It would appear that Mr. Hank Aaron did—not allegedly— but did in fact hit home run number seven hundred and five against Saint Louis Cardinal pitcher, Mr. Reggie *Cleveland*."

Sam almost swallowed his toothpick. Bert's hole disappeared. "Damn!" Sam muttered. Bert rubbed his stomach and popped in a couple of Rolaids. Sam tossed his toothpick in the garbage barrel and gave Bert a dirty look. "This one'll stump him, you said."

"Well, how the heck was I supposed to know?" Bert shrieked. "Anyhow, I said Jake wouldn't get it right. Never said nothing about the walking baseball encyclopedia over there."

"Yaw'll can argue later," I said. "Pay up."

Jake shook his tiny body and laughed. "Boy knows his baseball. Yes indeed." He held out his bony hand. "I'll take any combination of dead presidents you got."

Sam muttered and dug into his pocket. He took out a five and pointed to Bert. Bert turned up his lip. "It was your idea in the first place," Sam told him.

"Oh, all right." Bert forked over five ones.

"Thank you kindly," Jake said, blowing smoke in Sam's face.

"So, Jake, what you getting all spruced up for?" I asked him.

"Probably got a hot one with Velma," Sam shouted.

Jake took out his cigar and flashed his tobacco-stained grin. "Sorry to disappoint you, Sammy boy, but there's a whole lot hotter'n Velma out there."

I thought about Mrs. Simmons. Wondered what she was doing. Also thought about what Luther said. I sighed.

"Woooh, boy!" Bert shrieked, not noticing Sam slipping another one of Bert's black checkers back onto the board. "Who's the feline victim tonight, Jake?"

"None of your damn business. But I will tell you she's a spitfire I met up in Flagstaff last week."

"Jake, you told me you went up there on business," Luther said, brushing Jake's red and white curls off his back.

"Yeah, monkey business," Sam snorted. I shot him a hard look. "Oh—sorry Hawk," he said, putting up his hands like I was gonna arrest him.

Jake glared at him. "Not that it's really anybody's business what I do. But if you has to know, I was selling some property up there. But being the irresistible man I am . . . well, one thing led to another . . . and—"

"Hello!" Bert shrieked.

We were all laughing when we heard the loud crash. Somebody had run their old Packard into the barber pole outside.

"Luther, what the—" Jake shouted, and started cussing. Luther had nicked Jake on the chin and blood spurted all over Jake's clean white shirt on the shiny hardwood floor.

"I'm . . . I'm sorry, Jake!"

"I'm . . . I'm . . . nothing! Don't just stand there boy. Get me a towel and some alky—and hurry up!"

Everybody except me started calling Luther "Nick" after that day because of what he did to Jake. Luther didn't like it at first, but it kind of grew on him. He even changed his shop slogan to say "Haircut and Shave in the Nick of Time." He had the shop sign changed to *Nick's Place*.

Thank goodness Delores Paine wasn't hurt. When Bert saw she was all right, he made her angry because he kept pretending like she had to have been hurt.

"Delores—your face—oh, no—your face!" he said.

He had us in stitches, but Delores was not amused in the least. Luther would snicker, but sober up when she looked his way.

Delores didn't have a scratch on her, but that Packard didn't have a prayer. It was totaled for sure. She practically demolished Luther's barber pole. Took Luther almost a month to get it replaced. I told her a few weeks ago her brakes sounded strange. But she was stubborn. Said she ain't never had a colored man work on her car, and she wasn't about to start now. Her husband had passed away last year and she kept trying to get Luther to work on her car. Probably work on more than her car. She knew full well Luther only knew how to change a tire and put water, oil and gas in a car—that's all. I told Luther, Delores' prejudice was gonna kill her one day.

Prejudice *was* killing folks in that town. It wasn't Delores, though. It had other names on its death list.

Sheriff Hickerwood was always Luther's first customer on the last Wednesday of the month. Sheriff was never on time. Luther just knew Sheriff would be late for his own funeral when the time came. He said folks would probably get tired of standing around waiting for the mortician to bring the Sheriff's body, and they'd end up just burying an empty casket. One thing was for sure. Luther knew Sheriff would be exactly forty-five minutes late. He strolled into the shop at 9:45—right on the dot. He had his newspaper rolled up under his arms. His uniform shirt looked like his belly was begging for more room, hanging just over his belt.

"Hey, Nick," he called, taking off his ten-gallon hat. His hair had gone all white. His face was blotched with age spots. Luther glanced at the clock.

"Sorry I'm a bit late. It's busy over there."

Luther nodded.

"I don't understand this so-called lawyer in town," Sheriff said, peering at Luther through his glasses. "That black boy been here a good while now and he still don't know his place."

"What place is that?"

"You know. Now he's got everybody stone crazy, talking about defending that black boy, Danny Taylor. You know, the one we arrested for raping and assaulting little Tammy Hayes, the Reverend's daughter."

I think everyone in town had heard the story going round. Not that many of us black folks thought Danny had done it.

"I seen Tammy lately. There's nothing little about her." And he made a round across his stomach with his hands.

Sheriff Hickerwood scrunched up his face. "I'm not talking about her being in the family way. Course she wouldn't be like that if Danny—"

"Now, Sheriff," Luther said, "he hasn't been convicted yet."

He glared at Luther. "That boy is guilty. I know it. The whole town knows it. And you best be knowing it too. Besides, that Simmons is not even a criminal lawyer."

Luther shrugged. "How's the investigation going?"

"If you ask me there's nothing to investigate. Reverend Carl Hayes says Danny raped his daughter. I've known Carl all my life.

And a man of God don't lie. Besides, Danny was seen with her the day it happened."

"You mean the day she said it happened."

Sheriff Hickerwood spun around and Luther almost nicked his glasses. "What are you, some kind of expert in legal matters now?"

Luther shrugged again. "Nope. Just think you supposed to be innocent until somebody proves you guilty."

"Hmmph," Sheriff muttered. "If you ask me, lawyers just slow up justice getting done. Never met a one that was worth two cents. And whose side you on anyway?"

Luther took off the apron and brushed the hairs off Sheriff Hickerwood's red neck. "Not on no side. Just don't feel you ought to convict somebody before you got all the facts, that's all." He held up the mirror for Sheriff Hickerwood. Luther told me he wondered if folks actually recognized the face of prejudice when they saw it staring back at them.

Sheriff Hickerwood shoved the mirror back at Luther. "Now you went from being a simple barber to being an investigator, then a lawyer, now a lawman. You trying to tell me how to do my job?"

"Course not." Luther placed the mirror back on the shelf and smiled. "I heard Tammy Hayes been messing around with a man over in Casa Grande—a married one, I hear. Folks say she's pregnant with *his* baby."

Sheriff Hickerwood glared at Luther. Then he dug deep into his pants pocket and slammed fifty cents down on the counter. He took off his specs and blew the stray hairs off of them. "I think you ought to stop listening to idle gossip—stop believing everything you hear." With that, he grabbed his hat.

Luther looked at the clock as Sheriff Hickerwood stormed out. It had taken three days for most of the white folks in town to convince themselves that Danny Taylor was guilty. It took Sheriff Hickerwood fifteen minutes to try to convince Luther—to no avail. Luther sighed. He wondered how long it would take for the jury to yell out for Danny's blood.

Chapter Six

It was so quiet in that little courthouse the next morning you could hear the crickets making love outside. The cooler was blowing air, but everybody was still hot and sweaty. Looked like the whole town showed up for the hearing. Luther said hell's fire wouldn't have kept everybody away from that trial. It was Halloween. Perfect day for a witch hunt.

Judge Bufford's bald head was red, shiny, and piled up with sweat beads. He kept tugging at the collar of his stiff white shirt. Mr. Simmons must have been making Sheriff Hickerwood and District Attorney Porter nervous, because every once in a while Sheriff Hickerwood would rub his badge like it might be the last time he was going to get to wear it, and Porter would groan and run his hairy white knuckles across his round lips every time Mr. Simmons objected and Judge Bufford sustained it—which wasn't too often. Luther said watching Mr. Simmons was better than watching Perry Mason in action.

Every once in a while Danny would turn around and look at his mama and daddy sitting behind him. Mr. Taylor would send him a reassuring look, and his mama had her eyes closed most of the time. I knew she must have been praying. Danny kept rubbing his shoulder and fidgeting in his seat. Looking at how dark his mama and daddy were compared to Danny's yellow face, I knew my mama and Mabel were probably right about Mrs. Taylor fooling around with somebody else. But they were still married after all those years, and they both still supported Danny.

Luther had said he thought it was strange that Danny wasn't the same skin tone as his parents.

"Not really. Black folks have all color of kids. That's why you white folks call us colored."

Luther nodded. "So sometimes you get the same colors and sometimes you get a different one."

"That's right. I think it has something to do with the genes."

Luther scrunched up his face. "Their jeans?" he said. I had changed the subject while he thought a while on that one.

Jake Phillips was quiet all through the trial. Luther said it was the first time he'd ever seen Jake go that long without a smoke. Nobody even got up to the use the bathroom. None of us wanted to get the information second-hand from my mama Lucille and Mabel. We had to be there.

The silence was broken when Porter called the Reverend's daughter to the stand. There was some whispers and giggles, some gossipy chatter, and some moans and groans. Luther said Tammy Hayes put on the worst performance he'd ever seen. Her ash-blonde hair was brushed back into two ponytails down to her broad shoulders. She didn't have on the red and purple-colored makeup on her pudgy cheeks and eyes, like she usually did. But this was one time she needed it because the right side of her face was all black, blue, and swollen. Somebody had wopped her good.

Luther whispered that he recognized the pink and white granny gown with ruffles around the bottom Tammy was wearing. Delores Paine wore it the year before at the annual church picnic. He didn't like it when Delores wore it, and he thought it looked stupid on Tammy.

Well, Tammy Hayes poured out her story. You never heard so much blubbering and carrying on—except the time Bert got so drunk he thought that Indian statue in front of his drug store was a woman, and he went to bawling because she wouldn't talk to him.

After Tammy finished lying to all of Porter's questions, Mr. Simmons cross-examined her. But after a while it was obvious

Tammy was examining Mr. Simmons—with her greedy little hazel eyes. She dropped her baby voice and started twirling her long stringy hair. Luther said it was then that he thought the D.A.'s case had kicked the bucket.

Mr. Simmons started talking real sweet to Tammy, and boy did she respond! Mrs. Simmons must have noticed how Tammy was devourin' Mr. Simmons with her eyes, but she didn't seem angry or upset. Fact is I couldn't tell anymore what Mrs. Simmons was thinking. Luther said Mr. Simmons, on the other hand, told you exactly what was on his mind. And he didn't hold anything back that day in the courthouse—all the while twirling his tennis ball in one hand and holding his glasses in the other.

"Miss Hayes," Mr. Simmons called to her, "it appears you are not as fearful of black men as you testified earlier."

Tammy looked over at her daddy. "Well . . . you're not about to attack me like . . . like Danny did," she blubbered.

"So you still contend that Danny attacked you, is that right?"

"Yes, it was awful. I already said that."

"Yes, you did, didn't you? In fact, you said a lot of things, Miss Hayes. Now, I know this whole ordeal is very upsetting, so if you'll bear with me a few minutes more, I promise you it'll all be over."

Mr. Simmons went and sat on the table where Danny was sitting. Tammy never once looked Danny's way. "Miss Hayes, my client asserts that he never had sexual relations with you."

"He's a liar!" Tammy screamed, "A black boldface liar!"

Mr. Simmons was taken aback. She looked like Doris Day, freckles and all, but had the disposition of Doom's Day. "Ah," he said, "but it is your word against his."

Tammy turned her nose up. "All I know is what he did to me."

"Okay, Miss Hayes, let's just say that hypothetically, Danny did attack you."

Tammy gave him a look. She probably didn't know what "hypothetically" meant, but she took a deep breath, and sat up with a satisfied look on her face.

"Now, you said he struck you very hard and forcefully with his fist. That is what you told the police, isn't it?"

"That's right, that's what he did."

"So tell me, with which hand did he strike you?"

"Which . . . hand? Well . . . I don't know . . . what difference does it make? I just know he hit me!" She burst out crying.

Porter jumped up. "Your honor, this man is obviously and brutally badgering the witness. She's already given her statement to the Sheriff. We have it in writing. Why she's—"

Mr. Simmons sighed. "Your honor, if you will please bear with me, I have a very good reason for this line of questioning."

Judge Bufford frowned and rubbed his bald head. "Very well, Mr. Simmons." He waved Porter to sit down. "Objection overruled." He then turned to Mr. Simmons. "Just hurry up and get to the point, counselor. It's too damn hot in here."

Mr. Simmons turned to Tammy. "Now, Miss Hayes, you told Sheriff Hickerwood that Danny hit you with his knuckles across the right side of your face. Is that correct?" Tammy glanced over at her daddy again and then over at Sheriff Hickerwood, but she didn't say anything. "Miss Hayes, do I need to repeat the question?"

"Yes, I guess that's what I said. I really don't remember. I was frightened and upset."

Mr. Simmons opened up a manila folder. "Should I read your exact words from the report?"

"I said yes, that's what happened!" Tammy tossed her head. "Now leave me alone!"

Mr. Simmons seemed to always keep a safe distance away from her. He walked over in front of her. "I wish I could, Miss Hayes, but a boy's life appears to be at stake." He then turned to face Danny. I saw Mrs. Simmons smile and give him a nod. "So you say Danny struck you with his right fist on the right side of your face." He went over and picked up some papers off the table where Danny was sitting. "Your honor, I'd like to offer Dr. Peterson's medical report as Exhibit B, if I may."

Judge Bufford examined the papers and handed 'em back to Mr. Simmons who gave them to Velma, the Court Clerk.

"Now, Miss Hayes, it is vital that you make the jury and me completely understand your statement." He turned back to Tammy. "Miss Hayes, would you mind demonstrating for us the actual *motion* that you say Danny used to so brutally strike you."

"Objection, your honor," said Porter. "This man is wasting everybody's time. How many times does little Tammy have to keep reliving that awful incident? She's said the same thing time after time. Maybe this man should have his ears examined seeing as he can't hear too well."

A lot of the folks in the courthouse started laughing. Mr. Simmons clinched the ball in his hand. Judge Bufford went to bamming on the desk and calling for "order in the courthouse."

"Mr. Simmons, please indulge me by explaining."

"First of all, your honor, that is the seventh time the district attorney has referred to me as 'this man'. And since seven *is* the number of completion, I respectfully ask that *Mr.* Porter address me by my proper name. And second, it is vital to my client's defense that Miss Hayes demonstrate exactly how she was attacked. I assure you, your honor, I am definitely *not* wasting anyone's time!"

Judge Bufford glared at him. "I advise you, Mr. Simmons, not to raise your voice in this courtroom when you are addressing me."

"I'm sorry, your honor."

Judge Bufford nodded, rubbed his head again, and then pulled on his collar. "All right, I'll allow it. Objection overruled. And, John, please address the defense attorney by his surname, if you will."

Sheriff Hickerwood had a smirk on his face, but Porter looked like he was disgusted. I could hear Jake sucking his teeth. Mr. Simmons walked over to Tammy. "Miss Hayes . . ."

Tammy stood up and let out a big breath. "All right! He struck me like this!" She made a punching motion with her right fist.

"You're sure?"

"Yes."

Mr. Simmons copied her motion. "He hit you like this with his right fist?"

"Yes."

"Very hard?"

"Yes."

Mr. Simmons went over to the desk and picked up some photographs. "So hard he put these bruises on your face?"

Tammy rubbed her cheek and glanced over at her daddy. "Yes."

That's when most of us guessed it was probably her daddy who put those new bruises on her face. Come to think of it, he probably put those on her face a few months prior to this also—at least that's what my mama Lucille said later. I thought Mr. Simmons was gonna bring it up, but he didn't. Maybe he thought it wouldn't help his case if he was the one to accuse a church minister of beating his daughter. Mr. Simmons paused long enough to let the thought sink in with the whole court, then went on questioning Tammy.

"But what makes you so sure he hit you like this, Miss Hayes? As you yourself stated, you were very upset and remembered very little about the incident."

"I . . . I remember 'cause his big ugly elbow was pointed right in front of my face."

"Big?" Mr. Simmons said, raising his thin eyebrows. "Miss Hayes, I believe Danny Taylor is only five feet five inches tall, and weighs only a hundred and twenty-two pounds."

Tammy shrugged and tugged at one of her blonde curls. "Well, maybe not big. But his black ugly elbow was pointed right in front of my face. I was scared to death he was gonna kill me!"

There were whispers and murmurs in the courtroom. "You're positive about this?"

"Yes."

"Absolutely one hundred percent sure?"

"I said, yes I am!"

Mr. Simmons was standing in front of Tammy with his back to Danny. "That's very interesting, Miss Hayes . . ."

Before you could say "a-men," all in one motion Mr. Simmons turned and hurled a fast ball in Danny's direction. There was some "oh's" and "ooh's in the courtroom. Danny stood up and caught the ball in his left hand as if he'd been waiting for it. He was the best catcher we had during our softball games. Danny tossed the ball back to Mr. Simmons. Mr. Simmons then turned to Judge Bufford.

"Your honor, careful checking will confirm that Danny Taylor is, and always has been, unable to lift his right arm above his waist. He's been deformed since birth. There is no way he could have attacked Miss Hayes as she stated."

With that Mr. Simmons sat down. Luther thought it was a sure victory, but he couldn't understand why Mr. Simmons didn't have a smile on his face. Mr. Simmons just sat there with a stony look like he was waiting for the other shoe to fall. There was a lot of commotion in the courtroom and then silence again. Judge Bufford turned to Porter. Porter wrinkled his lip and then he smiled smugly. He strolled over to Danny with his fingers in his pockets. He then turned to the jury.

"It seems Mr. Simmons has done a bit of homework. He's pretty good at courtroom entertainment also, I see." He then smiled at Tammy whose mouth was hung open, and eyes as big as Sheriff Hickerwood's belly.

"Now, Miss Hayes, we understand that you may have been confused by which *hand* the defendant hit you with. That's understandable."

"Objection, your honor," Mr. Simmons blurted out in a monotone voice. "Counselor is leading the witness."

Judge Bufford stared at Mr. Simmons like he was getting tired of him. "Objection overruled," he said, and turned to Porter. "Continue."

Mr. Simmons stared straight ahead like he wasn't surprised that Judge Bufford had overruled him.

Porter smiled. "Tell me, Miss Hayes—in fact, tell the whole jury—did Danny Taylor rape you with either of his *hands?*"

With that, there was a round of guffaws and knee-slapping. Even Judge Bufford's face wrinkled. Mr. Simmons and the rest of us were not amused. Luther's eye twitched. Jake had his eyes fixed dead on Mr. Simmons. Judge Bufford decided he better restore order and bammed his gavel on the desk a few times. Things quieted somewhat. Mr. Simmons didn't bother to object. His head was down reading over some papers. Porter knew he had him now.

Tammy was sitting up higher in her seat. "I remember, it was his left hand he hit me with, and that was the hand he used to push me down—and then he assault . . . he struck me, just like I said."

Porter waved his arms from Tammy back to the jury and to the crowd, like he was directing traffic to proceed straight ahead. He then bowed as the crowd started clapping and laughing again. "No more questions," he said to Tammy. "You've been an excellent witness. Thank you," and he strolled back to his seat.

Tammy smiled and turned up her nose at Mr. Simmons.

Judge Bufford raised his eyebrows and looked at Mr. Simmons. "Uh, counselor, would you like to re-cross?"

Mr. Simmons took a breath. "No, your honor, I have no further use—I mean, I have no further questions for Miss Hayes."

"You may step down, Miss Hayes," Judge Bufford told her.

Tammy sashayed to her seat. It was quiet as all eyes were on Mr. Simmons. He looked over at Mrs. Simmons and Danny's parents. I saw Mr. Simmons give his wife a wink. She smiled. He got up.

"Your honor, I call Ella Mae Hickerwood to the stand."

You should have heard all the gasps. He was calling the Sheriff's sister, the only midwife in Coolidge besides Carolyn Johnson. Carolyn was a black midwife and delivered most of the black folks' children, but Ella Mae was called in when Carolyn was sick or out of town, or if some problems came up.

Me and Luther, along with everybody else, watched Ella Mae quietly walk to the seat. She was a small mousy-type woman who never got into anybody's business. She would sit quietly in church without saying a word. Luther said most of the time he didn't even know she was there. Luther leaned forward in his seat as Deputy Parker swore her in.

"I do," her quiet voice said.

Luther said he could tell she was scared. She would be going against her own brother. But we all respected her because she was good honest people.

Mr. Simmons smiled at her. "Miss Hickerwood, you are the registered nurse at Florence Hospital, is that right?"

She nodded.

"You have to answer verbally, I'm afraid," Mr. Simmons told her.

"Oh," she said, clearing her throat. "I mean, yes, that's right. I am."

"How long have you been a registered nurse?"

"Well, it's going on thirty-two years now, I believe."

"Thirty-two years?" Mr. Simmons said, turning to Porter. "I'd say you're pretty well grounded and knowledgeable in your field."

She smiled shyly. "Yes."

Porter must have been getting restless. He started scratching the big hairy mole on his chin.

"You also are a certified midwife. Is that correct?" Mr. Simmons asked Ella Mae.

"I am. I've delivered quite a few of those in here. Of course they were much smaller at the time."

Some of the black folks in the courtroom let out a giggle, as if glad to release some of the tension.

Mr. Simmons went over to his desk and picked up the papers he had been reading. "Your honor, I'd like to offer this sixteen-year-old medical report as Exhibit C, if I may."

Porter got up. "Your honor, how can a medical report from sixteen years ago be relevant to the case in point today? Is counselor going to perform one of his ball-throwing tricks again?"

Judge Bufford looked at Mr. Simmons to answer the question. Mr. Simmons sighed. "Your honor, this report proves that Danny Taylor could not possibly have raped Tammy Hayes." There were some murmurings that quickly quieted as Judge Bufford looked at the report. He gave Porter a sad look. "I'll allow it."

"May I see that, your honor?" Porter said, going over to the bench. He examined the papers, let out a big sigh, and then cast his eyes down toward Reverend Hayes. He straightened his tie and walked back to his seat.

Mr. Simmons handed a copy of the paper to Ella Mae. She looked at the paper as if recognizing it. "Miss Hickerwood, did you deliver Danny Taylor when he was born?"

Ella Mae smiled. "Yes I did."

"Is that your signature on the medical report at the bottom?"

"Yes it is."

"Is it true that Danny Taylor had polio as a child?"

"Yes."

"Is it also true that this same dreadful disease, that left him void of the use of his right arm, also left him with another, as yet incurable, malady?"

"I'm afraid it did."

Mrs. Simmons smiled at her husband. He went on. "Would you please tell us in your own words what that malady is?"

Ella Mae looked over at Sheriff Hickerwood. She wrinkled her lip and sighed like she wished she didn't have to be there. "The polio affected vital internal organs and the pituitary glands."

"Which means—?"

"Which means he would never . . . well, he would never be able to father a child."

The courtroom was beside themselves. Porter gave Reverend Hayes a disgusted look. Sheriff Hickerwood was glaring at Mr. Simmons. Reverend Hayes hid his face in his hand, while his daughter Tammy was just sitting there red-faced and breathing hard. A glimmer of a smile starting to appear on the black folks' faces, but they tried not to show too much emotion. I could tell they were like me—holding their breaths—waiting for the other shoe to fall.

Mr. Simmons continued. "So, in your expert opinion, Miss Hickerwood, could Danny Taylor have raped Tammy and now be the father of the child she is carrying?"

Ella Mae shook her head and smiled at Danny. "I'm afraid he could not."

Mr. Simmons sat down. Porter hemmed and hawed for a while. "No questions, your honor," he called out, putting up his hands in resignation.

When the jury came back in with a "not guilty" verdict, the whole courthouse was restless and in a uproar. Folks was calling each other names and issuing death threats to Danny and Mr. Simmons. Tammy Hayes was blubbering. I think my mama and Mabel was taking notes for the next gossip session. Judge Bufford was yelling and bamming on that worn out gavel, trying his best to restore peace and order. Look like the Civil War wasn't ever going to end—least not for Pinal County. And, what was worse, Luther said his eye was twitching.

Two days later, they found Danny dead just outside Florence. His tiny yellow body had been mutilated, almost beyond recognition. His scull was caved in, and he looked like he'd been tied up and dragged several miles. In the process, it must have broken his neck. I threw up when I saw the body.

Danny's mama, Ardell Taylor, kept screaming "I knew it! I knew it! Oh, my baby! My poor baby!" when we told her what happened. She sat on the floor for almost an hour like she was half-dead. Then her eyes were wild like an animal. She grabbed the big butcher knife on the counter and started heading down the road. We knew she was headed for the Reverend Hayes' place. It was almost a mile away, but we knew if we'd have let her she would have run all the way, and had energy left over. Mr. Taylor caught her and she swung the knife wild-eyed at him. It nicked his shoulder and blood spurted out.

He kept reaching for the knife. "Now, Ardell, you calm down!" he yelled at her.

"It's your fault!" she shouted at him, still swinging the knife. "If you hadn't been so stupid—you knew Danny wasn't your boy— you knew it—you never said nothing—nothing—"

"Ardell—please—give me the knife!"

"You didn't care who I did it with—long as you could have who *you* wanted—"

Then she let go the knife, blood on her hands and dress. She grabbed at her empty stomach and rubbed her empty womb. She let out a long, loud cry like she was giving birth. Then she dropped to her knees. "Ohhhh, I want my baby! I want my baby!"

Mr. Taylor hugged her and carried her back down the road to the house. Most of us stood looking. Danny's mama had acted on what we all was feeling. Most of us had hoped she would cut everybody and anybody who was responsible for killing Danny— until they looked like Danny's body. I realized Danny was us. Danny's mama was our mama. Her whimper was ours. Her moan was ours. We could hear her cries slowly die, seeping out like every ounce of hope we once had. We'd won—but Danny had lost.

All the black folks boycotted town. Luther closed up shop for a few days. It took several glasses of warm milk to calm his nerves. We didn't talk for at least a couple of weeks. He counted on losing a few customers. He said he didn't count on losing his friend. But he understood.

Three days later, Mr. Simmons, Danny's daddy, and a truck-load of us, including Mrs. Simmons, came barreling into town. Luther followed Jake and the rest of the men folk down the road. They stood out there looking. Jake still had shaving cream spread across his face. They watched as we stormed into the Sheriff's office. Mr. Simmons demanded that Sheriff Hickerwood get started on finding out who killed Danny. Sheriff Hickerwood didn't like folks busting into his office, and "nobody, but nobody, demanded nothing from him except to be locked up," he said.

"Who the hell do you think you are, boy?" he sneered at Mr. Simmons.

"I insist that you investigate this, Sheriff," Mr. Simmons said. I noticed Mr. Simmons didn't have his tennis ball with him.

Sheriff Hickerwood's veins began to pop in his neck. Then all of a sudden he leaned his chair back against the wall and clasp his hands behind his square-shaped head, and smiled. You could see the large sweat stains under his armpits.

"Now look here, Simmons, we all are about as torn up as you folks about what happened to that poor boy. But seeing as he *was* guilty, maybe justice has been done in spite of that jury's error in judgment."

Mr. Simmons' eyes tightened and he clinched his fists. "I don't believe what I'm hearing! A boy was wrongly accused, ridiculed and thrown into jail for a crime he didn't commit, and then finally, rightfully acquitted of all charges." Mr. Simmons took a deep breath and unballed his fist. His voice cracked. "Then, he's tied up like a dog . . . the very life dragged out of him . . . every ounce of dignity choked out of him . . . and you, you sit there with no remorse."

Mrs. Simmons reached out like she was going to touch her husband, but she put her hand to her mouth and tears streamed down.

"And you have the audacity to tell me *justice* has been done!" Mr. Simmons was out of breath and his eyes were watering.

Sheriff Hickerwood's smile disappeared. "Seems like a lot of justice could get done if you fool lawyers would let us do our jobs."

Charlie Parker, the new deputy, snickered and chewed his gum. Sheriff Hickerwood turned to him. "Charlie, this ain't a laughing matter. Simmons is right. That boy deserved to die with dignity. We'll see what we can do next time." Then he turned to Mr. Simmons. "Now yaw'll just run along like good boys and tend to your—"

He didn't get to finish. Mr. Simmons lunged at him, sending Sheriff Hickerwood up against the wall. Me and James Johnson grabbed Mr. Simmons' fists and dragged him off Sheriff Hickerwood. Charlie pulled out his pistol. Looked like they were going to arrest Mr. Simmons, but Sheriff Hickerwood waved to him to let him go.

"No need for that, Charlie," he said, smiling and brushing himself off. "I'm gonna let him pass this time because I can see how upset Mr. Simmons is. I think he just needs to go home and calm down—get a good night sleep." Then he sat back down and nodded toward Mr. Simmons and the other black folks. "Now you all get the hell out of my jail before I change my mind!"

We started pulling Mr. Simmons out the door. "I'm leaving," he said, pointing his long finger at Sheriff Hickerwood, "but I promise you, Sheriff, whoever is responsible won't go unpunished for this, if it's the last thing I do!"

Jake just shook his head. "C'mon, Nick, finish my shave. I got things to do."

We all went back over to Luther's shop and he finished shaving Jake.

"What you think Mr. Simmons gonna do?" Luther asked Jake.

Jake sucked his teeth. "Nothing, if he's smart. But then, he done already proved to me just how stupid he can be."

"Seems to me like they ought to find out who killed Danny," Luther told him.

Jake looked up at him with those cat-green eyes.

"Better watch what you say, boy. Don't be no fool like Simmons. He may be a smart lawyer, but right now his future ain't looking too bright."

Luther's stomach started bothering him. He was getting out his cutters, but Jake pushed them away. "Don't worry about a cut. I'll skip it this time. I got some business to take care of." He was still sucking his teeth when he left.

Several days later, Luther's eye was twitching so bad he had to put eye drops in. Around four that evening, Bert came barreling into the shop. "They set fire to the Simmons' house!" he shouted.

Luther locked up the shop. They all came trucking across town to the fire where we were. You could see the smoke dirtying up the sky. The air smelled like burnt meat. Some of us had already formed an assembly line, sweating and passing buckets of water— trying like the devil to put out the blaze. Strangest thing— somebody had cut the water hoses in half so we had to pass water buckets back and forth.

Luther kept wondering what was taking that fire truck so long to get there. They weren't any further away in town than from where he'd come. We knew the fire truck wouldn't get there in time.

It took us all of an hour to contain that fire. Folks was sweating, coughing, and wheezing. You could still hear wood crackling every few seconds. Luther saw the disgusted look on our faces when the fire truck came down the road, siren screaming. It was like rushing a drowning victim to the emergency ward after he's been under water for too many hours.

The firemen got out and waved us to stand back. "Anybody still in the house?" one of them asked. Before we could answer, they started moving boards that were still smoking. Everything they touched was breaking apart in their hands. We stood there staring into what remained of the Simmons place. The women—white folks and black folks alike—went to bawling.

After they moved some more of the boards, Delores Paine went to screaming. She was always overly dramatic. Even in church, during praise time, she'd jump up and start moving like she was feeling the Spirit. Luther said everybody knew she wasn't so much touched by the Lord as her girdle was riding up on her again. Anyway, she just wouldn't stop screaming. Velma had to slap sense into her. Luther said he wished it could have been him instead of Velma who did it, but he was standing too far away. But when Olivia went to screaming we had to forgive Delores for what we'd been thinking. We saw what she was screaming at.

Under some burnt wood were two charcoal bodies—nothin' but bone hanging out of burnt flesh. Olivia almost fainted, but I held on to her. I thought with her being a nurse she'd have been helping us instead. I felt my breakfast turning over inside of me. I saw a tear roll down Mr. Taylor's face when we came face-to-face with what we feared the most. Between what had to be Mr. Simmons' teeth, was his tennis ball. It had been dipped and set with an iron coating. Mr. and Mrs. Simmons had been tied up with chicken wire.

Apparently, somebody wanted to make a point. Mr. Simmons had served for the last time. He had aced them, but they made him and the rest of us eat crow—Jim Crow, that is. They had sent us a message—a chicken wire. They dared us to answer. I felt my knees go limp, but I was determined to stand up.

As if all this wasn't bad enough for their daughter, Alura, she lost her voice. I don't know if she tried speaking and couldn't, or never bothered to try. Maybe she could talk, if she put her mind to it, but no one ever heard her. That was when she started to do all this sign language, so I guess it was beyond doubt.

After we buried Mr. and Mrs. Simmons, Sheriff Hickerwood disappeared. He'd gone on a week vacation and didn't come back.

Charlie said Sheriff Hickerwood called and told him he was taking a week off, but he wouldn't say where he was going.

A month later, I still couldn't get the picture of Mr. and Mrs. Simmons out of my mind. We'd all been through a trying ordeal, but for the most part things were back to normal. Jake had let me ramble on about how Charlie and nobody in town was even trying to see that justice was done. He just puffed on his stogie, not saying anything for a while, just playing dominoes with Sam while Bert kept score. Luther was sweeping the floor and cleaning up. He knew Jake was bound to say something sooner or later.

"How old is you, Hawk?" Jake asked me, carefully laying down one of his domino pieces.

"What's that got to do with anything?" I shot at him.

He glared at me. "Now watch your tone, boy."

I put my head down and stared out the window.

"It's got everything to do with everything." Jake took out his stogie. "See, Hawk, a lot a folks call me a old fool 'cause I talk crazy sometime . . ."

"What you mean *talk* crazy?" said Sam. "And gimme five while he's talking," he called over to Bert.

Didn't seem to phase Jake. He just puffed on his stogie and laid down another bone.

"I learned a long time ago," Jake said, "life ain't always gonna be fair, and people sure as hell ain't gonna be, neither. Sometimes you gotta change the odds and make folks play your game. You understand what I mean?" He stuck his stogie back between his now hairy lips.

I looked over at him. His green eyes twinkled. Luther stopped sweeping for a moment and sat down, the broom between his legs resting on his stomach.

"Maybe *you* better find a game you good at," Sam said, smiling. He was winning. "Gimme another fifteen, Bert." He smacked his lips and slammed down another bone. They loved slamming them. It was like putting a exclamation point on the end of a good sentence. Luther said their punctuation was killing the heck out of his table.

I noticed they both had two bones apiece and it was Jake's turn. "Jake, you talking in circles," Luther muttered.

I sighed and took one of my chocolates out of my pocket. "*You* ain't got no idea how I feel," I said to Jake.

Jake looked up at me for a brief moment. "Maybe I do and maybe I don't. That ain't the point."

"Then what *is* the point?" Sam said, with a smirk.

Jake pushed his stogie to one side, got up and shoved his shirt inside his britches. He looked down at Sam, and then took out his stogie. I seen his eyes twinkle. "The point, you four-legged horny toad," he said, laying down one of his bones, "is first, you don't get old by being no fool."

Sam checked the board and cringed. He dropped his wrinkled forehead in his hand. Bert's eyes got wide and he rubbed his stomach. Jake pointed over to Sam. "Have some crow while you eating the rest of them bones," he said. Then he turned to Hawk. "And second, you beat the other sap while making him *think* he's one up on you." He slammed down his last bone while Sam was still pulling the last one from the pack and mumbling to himself. Jake grabbed the pile of money on the table and grinned. "And gimme *twenty-five* when I go," he said, winking over at me.

Bert shook his head and took a sip of beer. Then he snickered when Sam started cussing. Sam shot Bert hot looks across the room while Jake waddled out the door.

"What's so damn funny?" Sam shouted.

"Nothing," Bert laughed. "Not a thing. Care for a game of checkers?" Then he started rolling on the floor. Luther was giggling but he kept watching Sam, hoping he don't turn over the table. Sam was a poor loser.

"You got something to say, Nick?" he growled at Luther. Luther stifled his laughter and went to sweeping.

I smiled as I watched Jake waddle to his car. Luther didn't know, but Jake told me that day—in not so many words—what he'd done for Mr. and Mrs. Simmons, Danny, Danny's mama and daddy—and the rest of us. Me and nobody else really had any proof at the time, but I just knew. Jake had taken care of Sheriff Hickerwood. No, Sheriff Hickerwood would never show up alive. Don't know exactly what Jake did, but I'd gained a whole new respect for him. I saw him through Luther's eyes for a change. No, I decided, it wasn't Jake who killed Willie Jackson. I kept feeling that now Danny, Willie, and the Simmons, were all going to finally rest in peace.

Chapter Seven

The Simmons' relatives had their bodies shipped back to New Orleans for the funeral. Things settled down in Coolidge somewhat. Bert was reading the paper. Every once in a while between me and Jake's conversation, and Bert making faces, Bert would yell out "Jack Ruby done shot Oswald," and "Hey, Hawk, they might just pass that Civil Rights Law." John Glenn had spent a five-hour trip in space and John F. Kennedy had been killed. All Jake seemed to want to talk about is whether or not man had a soul.

Luther usually didn't mind when we got into deep discussions. He just worried about my son Tommy Lee. Tommy Lee was deaf to the world but he could read lips pretty well. And Tommy was afraid of Jake. Luther gave Tommy Lee a job running errands for him. Tommy Lee was cleaning out the store room, but every once in a while he peeked his head through the door just to make sure everything was all right.

"Ain't no such thing as spirits," Jake said, taking another swig of Johnnie Walker. "When you dead, you dead!"

"Jake, you may know a lot about life, but you don't know didley about dying," I told him. I'd started smoking cigars like Jake. Now Luther had two puff machines to put up with.

Jake burped. "Know all I wanna know. You all walk around praying and carrying on when times get bad like it's something that ain't 'sposed to be. I'm realistic. You got good times and you got bad times. Keeps things balanced."

"Oh yeah, well what's so balanced about a little baby dying for no reason in they crib one day, huh? Now explain that!" I shot at him.

Jake puffed silently on his stogie and everybody got real quiet. I turned toward Luther who was over by the sink cleaning his combs.

"Oh . . . Luther, I'm sorry . . . I didn't mean . . ."

Luther tried to smile and waved his hand. "I know you didn't mean anything," he said, drying the combs. "I think I'm gonna have to agree with Jake, though. I know death is part of living. I don't know about balance and all of that, but I believe God does things or lets things happen for a reason. His ways not like ours—like the Bible says."

I puffed and grinned, and gave Jake a wink. "Wooh, and all this time, Luther, I thought you just went to church to listen to my mama and Mabel gossip about folks!"

Bert was still making ugly faces and rubbing his big belly like he was in pain. I thought he was going to give another report, but his head was buried. I could hear clicks in his throat.

Jake grunted and coughed. "Well, I got a hard time believing a book that don't make sense *and* was wrote by a man, and I know not a one of them can be trusted."

I stubbed out my cigar in one of Luther's new ashtrays. I usually could only smoke about a third at a time. I wrapped it up in the tin foil I had in my pocket and nodded over to Luther. "What was that Reverend Hayes said that time?"

"About what?"

"You know, that man got what they wrote from God."

"Well, kind of, yeah . . . I guess you could say man was inspired by God. God told them what to write and when to write it."

"Yeah, by his Holy Spirit," I said, satisfied. I smiled over at Jake. Luther said I resembled my mama when I closed my eyes and leaned back in my chair with my arms folded.

"Hmph! Only spirits I care about is this," Jake snorted, holding up his bottle.

"Don't you wanna go to Heaven, Jake?" Luther asked.

Jake's green eyes dimmed a little. "Heaven? Boy, you don't even know what it is." Before Luther could answer, Jake pointed his bottle at me. "You wanna get to Heaven?"

"Sure do," I said, leaning back and putting my hands behind my head.

Jake's eyes twinkled. "Uh-huh. Well, you wanna die?"

I thought a moment. "No. Do you?"

Jake laughed. "I rest my case. If that place supposed to be so fine and dandy, tell me how come none of yaw'll so-called God-fearing Christian folk wanna die to get there? Now answer me that?"

Bert put down his newspaper. "Listen, can we change the subject," he said, and then made a dash for the toilet.

Jake smacked his lips. "Must be the Lord working in one of his *mysterious* ways!" he said, arching his hairy eyebrows up at Luther.

I reached over and picked up the paper Bert was reading. My voice grew kind of hollow. "No wonder Bert's stomach is so upset."

"What's that?" Jake asked, hugging his bottle.

"Some folks found Sheriff Hickerwood in his cabin up in Prescott," I said.

"Oh?"

"Hanging from a rope. A few weeks ago."

Luther almost dropped his pail.

I nodded. "Said it looked like suicide, but they didn't find no suicide note."

Tommy Lee was standing in the doorway watching us. I could tell he sensed something was wrong.

"Finished?" I formed with my lips. He nodded. "We better get on home," I told Luther. When we got to the door, I turned to Jake. "See you later," I said.

He nodded without looking up.

Bert was just coming out of the bathroom. Jake tossed his bottle into the barrel. "Like I said, when you dead . . . you dead."

The Simmons' daughter, Alura, moved back to Coolidge shortly after Sheriff Hickerwood's memorial service. And she was still using this sign language. It surprised just about everybody in town that she came back, especially Luther. She bought old Papa Jo's house, located just across the road from Luther. Jake said he gave Alura a good deal because of what happened to her folks, but he didn't feel too comfortable about the whole thing, what with her being black. When Papa Jo was alive he wouldn't allow black folks within twenty feet of his property, if he could help it, and Jake sort of felt ashamed about it now.

The roof leaked, the screen door was off the hinges, tumbleweeds were scattered all across the dirt road, and the boards on the huge wooden porch looked as if they would give way any minute. She received enough insurance money from her parents' death, along with their savings and the money she'd saved from her job. She could have had a nicer home closer to town, but she made it plain to Jake that it was the one she wanted.

At first Luther only got distant glimpses of Alura. She looked like her mama, except she had her daddy's height. She drove a blue Plymouth. She didn't ask anyone in town to help her move. Looked like she hired out-of-state movers to do everything. Almost everything. Me, Olivia and Tommy Lee was over quite a bit at first. We helped her paint and fix things up.

Alura was one subject Luther steered clear of talking to me about. He wanted to know why she seemed to have different men visiting her all the time, but he didn't dare ask. But then all he had to do was sit behind Mabel and my mama, Lucille, and he learned more than he cared to.

It seems Alura and her huge welcome mat became the most talked about items in Pinal County. The church was unusually hot that day. The cooler was on the blink again, and there were too many bodies to make the feel and the smell of the air comfortable. Yes, hot with sweat and hot with gossip. Luther had a keen sense of hearing. I was sitting next to Olivia at the other end. All I heard were whispers.

"Musta taken that chile a whole year to stitch up that thang," my mama Lucille said, fanning herself.

"You done seen it, Lue?" Mabel asked, her eyes big as tires.

"Sho nuf. Got a orange-brown background with big yella letters on it spelling *WELCOME*, shaped like a bright rainbow, with four white daisies setting in the corners, and her first name *ALURA* spelt at the top, and her last name *SIMMONS* at the bottom, and *them* letters is stitched up in alternating colors of red and white. Can you believe it!"

"Go on, Lue!" Mabel whispered.

"It's true, Mabel. I 'member when she first started workin' on it. Musta been 'bout, what, a little over a year ago, right after her momma and daddy died."

Lucille looked up and shouted "A-MAN," to Reverend Hayes' sermon and then leaned back over towards Mabel.

"And, it's downright disgraceful how she been living, throwing her momma and daddy death money away on all those good-for-nothing, no-account, free-loading mans. She probably done played more ball in six months than Jackie Robinson gone play in the major league this whole year. I tell you, Mabel, if she ain't wore out, that mat oughta be!"

They both cackled, and Reverend Hayes sent them a look that quieted them for a few minutes. Then Mabel leaned back over towards Mama.

"That's jus' awful, Lue—pretty thing like that. She oughta settle down and marry up with a good God-fearing man. That's what she oughta do, if you ask me."

My mama Lucille gave Mabel a long saucy look and folded her long dark brown arms as she rubbed her sweat-stained back, indignant-like, up against the faded wooden benches. "Now how she gone do that? Won't step a foot inside church! And her mama and daddy both never missed a Sunday." My mama pursed her red lips. "Well I tell you, Mabel, *I personally* went over to get her to come with me last Sunday."

"What she say, Lue?"

"What she say? What do you think she said? Didn't see her last Sunday, didja?"

"Naw . . ."

"Didn't say nothing, like always. Just wrote me one her notes—very proper too—course she graduated from college and all, you know. Note said: 'Thank you kindly for *offering*, Mother Williams, but the preacher gets my money every week, what does he need my body for?'"

Mabel's eyes got even bigger and her jaws dropped open. "Go on, Lue!"

"She even had the nerve to P.S. it. Said: 'And my soul is not up for grabs!'"

"Chile, hush yo' mouth!"

My mama closed her eyes and lips and nodded with her hat bobbing up and down, like she always did when she was real serious about something. "As God is my witness, Mabel—word for word. I saved it an' showed it to Reverend Hayes."

"Lucille!"

Mama saw Reverend Hayes' piercing stare. "A-MAN, brother!" she shouted, and leaned back over to Mabel. "Sure did. But, chile, I knowed he wasn't gone do nothing."

Lucille sat back up, like she was interested in Reverend Hayes' sermon.

Mabel stared at her, jaws wide open. "Lue?"

"Hmmm?"

"Lucille! What? What he say?"

"Oh yeah . . . so he says 'Well, Sista Williams, the Lawd works in mysterious ways. He's working on Sista Simmons' soul, and

God'll reach her one day. All we can do is pray for poor Sista Simmons.'"

"A-man to that! That little girl is gonna need it!" said Mabel.

Hmph," said Mama, "I say she's the devil's chile, that's what I say."

"A-MAN!!" the congregation shouted, as Reverend Hayes finally brought his sermon to a close.

Luther decided to reserve judgment on Alura. Some of the folks would make fun about how she majored in Communications at school but refused to speak a word. Luther couldn't imagine any woman going that long without talking. He knew ten minutes would send Delores Paine into convulsions. Ever since her husband passed, Delores would always come over to Luther's pretending to borrow something—usually a cup of sugar or flour. Luther didn't like folks borrowing things all the time. He put up with Delores because she'd offer to do his laundry. We asked him if they were dating. Luther said he thought Delores was just in love with his underwear.

Luther was cleaning up his yard when Delores came over to his house that afternoon. She was still dressed up in the same getup she had on earlier at church that day. Her orange high heels were making dents in his wooden porch. There was a peach-colored hat with a white feather on the side, propped on her head.

"Well, Nick, hello!" she said, like she was surprised to see him at his own house. She went to fanning herself with one of those oriental fans she sent away for out of the Dewey's catalog. "Sure is a hot one today."

Luther didn't look up. "Imagine that. Hot in July. In Arizona." He kept right on sweeping the porch.

Delores had her hands on her hips. "Well?"

"Well, what?"

"Nick, aren't you going to offer a lady a cold drink?" she said, batting her false eyelashes.

"Something wrong with the water at your house?"

Delores let out a laugh. "Oh, Nick, you're always kidding."

Luther told me he could smell lemons. He really hated lemons.

"Well?" she said. "Aren't you going to invite me in? I have to talk to you about something extremely important."

Luther decided she wasn't going away. He told me she reminded him of that fly he was chasing around the house the other day. It just kept pestering him to death. He ended up having to use capital punishment. He decided Delores was much too big to swat.

"Okay, Miss Paine, come on in. Have to excuse the place. As you can see, I'm trying to clean up."

Delores wrinkled her nose. "Nick, you shouldn't have to do this. Don't you know that cleaning is women's work?"

"Well, seems like I'm always doing work I'm not supposed to." He put down the broom. "You said you had something important to talk about?"

"Oh, yes I do," she said, sinking into his sofa. Just what he was afraid of—she was going to be staying a while. Luther kept wondering if they sold giant size fly swatters in that Dewey's catalog.

"Now, Nick, it's been at least fifteen years we've known each other, and you are still calling me Miss Paine. Why is that?"

Luther shrugged. "Out of respect, I guess," he said, and went to dusting the book shelves.

"Well, respect my wishes and call me Delores. You hear?"

"Okay, so what you run out of this time?"

She let out a phony cackle. "Oh, Nick! I didn't come to borrow anything. Now stop that cleaning for a moment and sit down. I want to talk to you."

Luther sighed and put down the cloth. The heat was making him tired anyway. He planted himself in Amanda's favorite chair just across from Delores.

Delores rubbed her double chin. "My throat is mighty dry. Can I trouble you for a cold drink?"

Luther got up and went into the kitchen. He looked in the ice-box. He had some root beer, but he poured her some ice water instead. He figured it was best to give her veins what they were used to. When he went back in she'd slipped off her pointy-toed shoes. The smell of lemons was closing in on him.

"Thank you, Nick, how sweet," she cooed, taking the glass. Luther watched her as she took a sip. "Oooh, that's good and cold. Just what I needed."

Luther snickered.

"What's so funny?"

"Nothing," Luther said, and propped the side of his face in his hand.

Delores set the glass down on the coaster. "So how you been, Nick? Been feeling all right?"

"Except for a few gas problems, I'm fine. Thanks for asking."

She grinned. "Oh, Nick," she said, putting her hand to her face like she was embarrassed. She took another sip and sniffed. "It's a bit disappointing Mr. Goldwater didn't get elected. Don't you think?"

"Well . . ."

"I think that election was fixed. What do you think?"

"Oh, well I . . ."

"Why there's not a better and sweeter human being on the face of this green earth. Don't you think so?"

"Well, you know . . ."

"All of Coolidge was behind him one hundred percent."

Luther was quiet.

"Did you hear me?" Delores was excited now.

"Uh-huh."

"Well, it is polite to answer when somebody's talking to you."

Luther shook his head. "I was just waiting for you to finish so I could talk."

Delores let out a phony cackle again. "Oh, Nick, you kill me. You simply kill me!"

Luther knew the offer was tempting, but he figured she'd be leaving sooner or later. "Fact is," he said. "I didn't vote for Goldwater."

Delores almost choked on her water, and she coughed. "What? Why I thought we all agreed at the town meeting . . ."

"You all agreed. I figured who I vote for is my own personal choice and my own personal business."

She gave him a look and then smiled. Luther must have seen at least a million teeth.

"Well, I guess that *is* true, Nick. Now I don't agree with your choice . . . but I guess I do have to respect your right to vote for anybody you choose to."

Luther leaned forward. "Well, that's right neighborly of you, Delores."

Delores played with the peach-colored pearls around her neck. "You mind my asking why you didn't vote for him?"

Luther shrugged. "Lot of reasons. The main one being I figure any grown-up man going around wearing them ridiculous 'Go-with-Goldwater' glasses is not somebody's hands I wanna be putting my state of affairs in."

Delores laughed. It was for real this time.

Luther snickered too. "Now I know you didn't come over here to discuss politics. What's on our mind?"

Delores caught her breath. "Well, all right." She reached in her large handbag and pulled out some papers and a pen. Luther said he thought she wanted him to donate some money to the women's auxiliary again.

She crossed her flabby legs, her wide skirt flared out. She straightened up her back, and her nose tilted way up in the air. "Now, Nick, you know I been living next to you for close to ten years. Amanda and I were always close, you know."

Luther grinned. "Far as I can remember, you two were always close to killing each other."

Delores pursed her orange-colored lips. "Well . . . anyway, as I was saying . . . it's been over fifteen years we been in this neighborhood, and it has always been a respectable place—"

"Near about, yeah."

"Well, all of us on the Women's Fellowship Committee would like your signature on this petition—"

"Petition? For what?"

Delores pointed out the screen door down the road. "To kindly ask Miss Simmons to vacate, what has been a decent and God-fearing town for at least twenty years!"

Luther got to his feet. "Don't sound to me like you're asking—sounds more like you're ordering."

Delores' face flushed. "We have had enough of her . . . well, her lustful ways!"

Luther glared at her. "The last time I looked this was a free country. Where you all get off telling folks where they can live? And far as I can tell, Miss Simmons never broke any laws here in town."

Delores' nose almost pointed to the ceiling by now as she stood up. Her hat teetered on her head. "Well, Miss Simmons may not have broken any of man's ill-begotten laws, but she sure has broken every divine law there is. Why, with her immoral and indecent conduct—"

"She seems pretty decent to me," Luther shouted at her. "Keeps her yard and place clean. She don't bother anybody. She never borrows anything from me. They say she donates to the church, and the fellas at the shop all like her—always saying good things about her."

Delores sniffed, and tossed her head back. "That's exactly my point! All the men like her—for obvious reasons that a lady like me won't dare talk about . . . but I know for a fact she commits fornication—playing around with anything moving with pants on it. Why, it's—"

Luther snatched up Delores' shoes and shoved them to her. He pointed her body toward the door.

"Why, Nick—" she said, flustered.

Luther was breathing hard. "If that don't beat all—the pot calling the kettle black. Miss Simmons keeps mostly to herself. She don't go snooping around and sticking her nose into everybody's business—like some folks!" He pushed open the screen door and held it. "Now good day, Miss Paine, before I get up a petition to have your jaws wired!"

"Well!" Delores gasped, hurrying out the door.

At least Luther didn't have to worry about her trying to borrow things from him anymore. She didn't speak to him any more after that. "Shoot," Luther told me, "God does work in mysterious ways!"

That following winter Alura came down with a bad case of the flu that was going around. Her being a tiny thing, it made her pretty weak. Probably too, Luther knew she didn't take very good care of herself. He saw her out on her porch, shivering and coughing while she covered up her plants so they wouldn't get soaked from the rain. Luther didn't see her for a few days after that, so he offered to pay Olivia to look in on her and do whatever needed doing. Olivia was a nurse now, over at Florence Hospital. If you remember, she was my Aunt Mabel's ex-husband's niece. Even I had to keep telling myself that one. Families can be kinda complicated. We were . . . well, we were seeing a lot of each other now.

"Oh, Nick, you don't have to do that," Olivia told him. Luther said Olivia's brown almond-shaped eyes and big cheeks made her look like a bunny rabbit. I love rabbits.

"But I insist," Luther told her. "Just don't tell Alura . . . or Hawk—you know, he might misunderstand."

Olivia smiled and nodded. She was real smart, and people liked her. Jake said she couldn't have been that smart, 'cause she was dating me. Olivia did tell me, but I swore I wouldn't let Luther know I knew. There were so many silly secrets, and don't tell him this and don't tell her that, and my mama and everybody gossiping. We could've started our own soap opera: "Stormy Secrets of Alura Simmons."

Alura paid Olivia to do her shopping and different chores around her house. Olivia told Luther that Alura said she wouldn't let Doc Peterson look in on her.

"You mean she talked to you?" Luther asked, surprised.

"No, Nick, she wrote it down." Olivia reached into her red handbag. "See . . ."

Luther took the note. Alura had very good handwriting—very neat. Sure a lot better than those scribbles he called letters.

Alura was straight and to the point with her message. Three lines:

"Don't like doctors.

Never have—never will.

Hands too cold."

Luther handed the note back to Olivia, and giggled. "So how's she doing?"

"Still a little weak, but as you can see from her notes she's still spunky as ever." Olivia laughed. "I swear, sometimes Alura has my sides splitting!"

Luther told me later he was feeling a bit nervous. "Well, what do you two find so God-all funny."

Olivia coughed and shifted her weight to the other side. "Oh, you know, just girl stuff. Nothing important."

Luther said he couldn't believe Alura would talk about "girl stuff"—whatever that was. She looked so serious most of the time.

I didn't talk much about Olivia to Luther at first, but he could tell I was crazy about her. Along with her round cheeks and almond-shaped puppy-dog eyes, she had a forceful speaking voice. Kind of like way Tina Turner sings.

Olivia was close to thirty, but she looked more like twenty. Mabel raised her along with her own six children because Olivia's mama was shot a long time ago by a jealous boyfriend. Luther decided he and Olivia had a little bit in common because both of their mothers died when they were young, and neither one of them knew their daddy. And far as the both of them knew, neither of them had any natural sisters and brothers.

Luther watched Alura and Olivia across the way that evening. Alura was curled up in a blanket and Olivia was preparing dinner for her. They got along real well. Olivia was about three years older than Alura. They looked so different but both had a beauty hard to miss. Olivia was tall and big-boned while Alura was short and small-boned. Alura had long thin curly hair pinned up in a bun, and Olivia had her hair in a short "natural." Luther said he didn't know the difference between what was supposed to be natural and unnatural. I explained it to him.

Olivia never had a sick day in her life as far as I can remember. Her being a nurse, Luther figured she knew how to take care of herself. But Alura—Luther wasn't so sure of. With that many fellas, he wondered she wasn't sick all the time.

Luther told Olivia to come over when Alura got well and he'd pay her. When Olivia came over, she had an envelope for *Luther* instead—from Alura. Said Alura already paid her.

Olivia gave Luther a reassuring look. "Honest, Nick, I didn't tell Miss Simmons. Honest, I didn't."

Luther read the note when Olivia left. It said: "Thank you, Sir Galahad."

Luther was sure glad to see Alura up and around again, but he said he'd be darned if she didn't have another gentleman caller over not too long after that. He caught sight of them kissing outside her porch one night. The porch light cast a spotlight on them, and Luther could see thick black arms wrapped tight around her tiny little waist. The man's face was buried in her neck. Luther said it reminded him of one of the vampires he'd seen on television the other day. He noticed the man's big black boots as they strolled across the porch into her house.

His stomach started bothering him like it did whenever he thought about Amanda, so he went in and put on some warm milk. Somebody knocked on his door. It was Jake.

"How you been, boy" Jake said, lightly slapping Luther on the back. Sounded like he had a chest cold.

"Jake, you old son of a gun, where you been? Haven't seen you in a few months."

"Had some business to tend to in New Orleans."

"Come on in. Join me in some milk?"

Jake screwed up his small face as he waddled in. "Damn it to hell, boy, you too young to be ailing with a nervous stomach. Better find you a gal and get married. She'll heal that right quick." He winked up at Luther. Jake seemed to be shrinking. Luther knew he wasn't getting any taller, so it had to be Jake was getting shorter.

Jake plopped down on the sofa and grinned. "Hear Delores Paine got eyes for you."

"C'mon, Jake, what you think made my stomach so nervous?"

Jake let out his deep throaty laugh. He looked around the room. "Ain't you got nothing stronger? Say, Johnnie Walker, maybe?"

Luther looked at him. "Guess there's no way I can talk you out of it, is there?"

"Nope," Jake said. His voice sounded a bit hoarse.

Luther went over to the cabinet where he kept liquor for company. He poured Jake a glass. "Here you go."

"Thanks, boy." Jake raised his glass to his puckered lips and took a sip. Luther noticed that his hand shook a little. He let out a big "aaahhh."

"Walk, Johnnie, walk!" Jake smacked his lips. "So what's been happening over yonder?" he said, pointing his bony chin up towards Alura's house.

Luther sat down across from him. "Well, she was ailing with the flu a few weeks ago. I got Olivia to take care of her and get her back on her feet again."

Jake sent Luther a stare colder than Delores' disposition. Those almond-shaped green eyes pierced right through him. Jake's high cheekbones rose a little higher as he sucked his teeth. "You ain't sweet on that little gal, is you?"

Luther looked down. "It's not that. I just care what happens to folks, that's all," he stammered out.

Jake was quiet for a few minutes and sipped his drink. Then he grinned. "Know what your problem is, boy? You a darkie-lover," he said, staring hard at Luther.

Jake's words pierced Luther's gut deeper then those green eyes of his had, but Luther decided to hold his peace. Jake just shook what few curls he had on his white head, and swallowed up the rest of his drink.

"I gotta go over and pick up the mortgage payment from that little gal," he said getting up. "See ya next Friday at the shop."

"Later, Jake."

Luther watched Jake as he ambled over to Alura's house. He looked like a penguin when he walked, because one of his legs was shorter than the other one. It was more noticeable now that he was getting older.

Luther smelled something burning. He remembered his milk. Darn thing overflowed—looked like plastic. He cleaned up the mess and thought about what Jake had said about finding somebody to marry. He hadn't really thought he'd get married again after Amanda.

Chapter Eight

Seems like Coolidge was always behind the times in everything. Silas Taylor, the Taylors' next-to-the-oldest-son, made a point to visit his cousins in Los Angeles every summer. He'd come back sporting the latest fashion and hairdo. All the girl Taylors had long coarse hair when Mrs. Taylor took a hot comb to it. The girls' hair and faces would be shining with grease—hair hanging down their back. Silas came home one summer wearing the biggest "afro" you ever wanna see. I put up with Olivia's, because it wasn't very much. Silas said everybody was wearing it like that in L.A. He even had on a dashiki and sandals. The rest of the guys was talking about "black power," giving high-fives, and all I heard was Eldridge Cleaver, Angela Davis, Huey Newton and the Black Panthers.

Luther and Jake were concerned with getting tickets to the Giants' game. The Giants were playing the Cubs in one of their spring training games. Jake knew somebody who knew somebody who got them tickets.

The drive from Coolidge to Phoenix was less than two hours. But since Jake was driving, Luther made sure to allow for three. Jake didn't seem to mind getting somewhere late, but it drove Luther crazy.

"Boy, we ain't but, what, fifteen minutes late," Jake would tell him. "Ain't nothing to get excited about."

"That's fifteen less minutes we have to enjoy the game," Luther called back to him. "A lot can happen in that time."

"In baseball?" Jake said, and then lit up a stogie.

Luther had to agree there. A score could stay 0-0 for at least fifteen minutes, but Luther was always determined to get to the games on time. So he'd tell Jake the game started an hour earlier than it did. After a while Jake caught on because they'd be one of the first ones there. Jake would carry on about how long it took the game to start. Then he'd notice that Luther didn't look too worried or even check his watch. Luther thought Jake was going to yell at him when he figured out what he was doing. But he didn't. He just started showing up at Luther's a half-hour *later* than the time Luther told him to pick him up.

Luther said the air smelled rain fresh on the drive to the game. It was just springtime and seventy degrees outside. Jake was a little too quiet that day.

"This is gonna be one heck of a game, Jake. Just wait."

Jake drove quietly, staring straight ahead. "Uh-huh."

"Think the Cubs are gonna be hard to beat?"

"Uh-uh."

Luther opened his window some more. "You tired?"

"Some." Jake was sounding more and more hoarse.

"Want me to drive?" Luther offered.

Jake shook his white head. "Wanna get there in one piece."

Luther sat there quietly looking at the cactus and wet dirt and rocks for a while. He'd known Jake a long time. "How come you haven't gotten married?" Luther asked him.

Jake scrunched up his face. "Now how we get all the way from driving to marriage?"

Luther smiled. "I don't know, just wondering."

They both sat there for a few minutes. Jake would cough every once in a while and spit out the window.

"How old are you, Jake?" Luther asked.

Jake grinned. "Old enough—why?"

Luther shrugged. "Just seems important right now, that's all."

"It ain't never seemed important before. But if you must know I'm seventy-seven—just two weeks ago."

Luther's eye twitched. He put his hand to his head. "Oh no, Jake, I'm sorry. I forgot."

"Forget it, boy," Jake told him. Then he looked over at Luther and tried to smile. "But I guess you done already did that."

Luther felt awful. Jake always remembered his birthday. Then he thought about it. Jake was getting up there in age.

"You been to see Doc lately?" Luther asked him.

Jake sat up and wrapped both his arms around the steering wheel like it was the only thing keeping him up. "What's with all these questions, boy?"

"Just want to make sure you're all right."

Jake rubbed his throat. "Yeah, I've been to see him. Ain't too sure he seen me though. He's about as blind as the Cubs' umpire." Then he let out a hoarse laugh. He noticed Luther looking at his hands. "Aw c'mon, boy—I'm about as good a shape as any near eighty-year-old Casanova who's been smoking, drinking, and you-know-whating all his life."

"You ought to take better care of yourself. Life's too short."

Jake rubbed his age spots on the back of his hands. "Hell, boy, you got to go someday anyhow. Why die healthy, I say?" He tried to laugh again, and the coughing got so bad he had to pull over. "Reach in there and hand me my pills," he said, pointing his bony finger at the glove compartment.

Luther hurried up and took out the bottle. He popped open the cap. "How many you supposed to take?"

"Gimme two."

Luther reached for the bottle of water under his legs and poured Jake some water in his *I love New Orleans* coffee mug. Jake shoved the pills inside his wrinkled lips and chewed. Luther hated when he did that, but Jake said he had a hard time swallowing any kind of pills, so he put up with the bad taste. He almost spilled the water trying to take a drink.

"Maybe I better drive," Luther told him.

Jake looked like he was going to object, but he moved slowly over to the passenger side. When they drove up to the stadium, Jake was looking better.

"Those pills for pain?" Luther asked.

"Nope."

The crowd was gathering, but the game hadn't started yet. Jake got out and looked around. Then he checked his watch. "What time you got?" he asked Luther.

Luther hesitated. "Oh—uh . . . a little after two."

Jake looked at him. "How little?"

A guilty smile crossed Luther's face. "Two-thirty," he said.

"The game didn't start at two," Jake said matter-of-factly.

"No," Luther said, looking at him, trying to see if he looked mad. "Three o'clock."

"Uh-huh," Jake said, and went and got back in the car, leaving the door open.

Luther walked around to Jake's side. "Aren't you mad at me?"

"You bet your porcupine behind I'm mad at you," Jake said. "That's why you gonna pay."

For the first time in over thirty-five years, Luther didn't enjoy the game. He kept worrying about Jake. Usually Jake carried on, saying things like "hang the ump," and yelled for the batter to "give the pitcher a close shave this time!" But he was strangely quiet. Luther figured since his eye wasn't twitching any more, there couldn't be anything seriously wrong.

Still, he had this nagging feeling down in his belly. Could have been the four hot dogs he stuffed down. But why did Jake have to smoke so much? Luther told me how he'd tried to smoke one time. Pete and Bo had talked him into it. He figured he'd try most things at least once. They had kept talking about how girls liked it because it made boys look cool. They told Luther he was chicken if he didn't try it.

They hid down in the basement at Bo's house. His folks were gone to Shopes. Luther didn't feel "cool" down in that hot basement. It had to be about a hundred degrees. He watched Pete light it up and take a big puff. He let out the smoke, trying to blow a ring. His eyes looked red, but he seemed to enjoy it. He handed it to Bo who took a few puffs and smiled as he let the smoke come out of his nose. He passed it to Luther who took a puff, coughed like crazy, and could hardly catch his breath. He felt sick to his stomach and his eyes hurt for a whole week. Both Pete and Bo had laughed.

Luther decided he didn't want to hang around with them anymore. He thought about how his mama never smoked a day in her life, but darn it if cancer didn't find another route in her body. The Giants lost the game two to six, and Luther lost ten bucks to Jake. When they were leaving, Luther's mouth hung open and his stomach churned like it did that day he'd taken a puff of that cigarette. There was a black man with his arms draped around a white woman's neck, and she had both her arms locked around his waist. They were talking and giggling. Luther stared at them when they started kissing.

"Boy, close your mouth and let's go find the car," Jake said, pulling at his arm.

They found Jake's old Mustang with no problem. Luther asked him why he didn't get a new car, seeing as he could afford it. Jake told him that 1965 Mustangs were considered classics and he didn't need another car. "You can have it when I'm gone," Jake said.

Both of them were quiet most of the drive home. Finally Jake spoke up. "First time you done seen that, I take it?"

"Huh?" Luther said. "Seen what?"

Jake motioned his head in the direction they just left. "You know, boy, darkies and whites—together like that."

"Oh, yeah," Luther said, with a stiff shrug. "I guess so."

Jake coughed. "You see a lot of that nowadays."

"Never seen it in Coolidge," Luther said, staring at him, wondering why Jake didn't seem so upset.

Jake let out a weak snicker and looked out of the corner of his eye at Luther. "Uh-huh. That you know about. Fact is," he said rubbing his chin, "sometimes a whole lot gets by you, boy."

Luther didn't like him saying that, but he guess Jake was right.

"Now I ain't saying you ain't smart. Just at times . . . well, you can be . . . naive." Jake patted him lightly on the back. "In your own little world, but you plenty all right with me."

Luther smiled. He put on the lights because it was getting dark outside. "Hey, Jake?"

"Yeah?"

"Why don't you like Alura Simmons?"

Jake looked over at Luther and sighed. "Ain't got nothing against that little gal."

"Then it must be her folks you didn't like? You got something against a black lawyer?"

Jake scrunched up his green eyes. "Why you so all fired up about it?"

Luther sat up. "Because she seems to treat people pretty good, and she could probably use all the friends she can get her hands on. Most women in town, except for Olivia, talk badly about her."

Jake sucked his teeth. "Don't seem to me she's too lonely."

"I don't mean those kinds of friends. I mean real friends." Luther looked over at him. "You know, Jake, like us."

Jake let out a throaty laugh and coughed a little. "Hell, then she ain't gonna be needing no enemies then—is she?"

"Oh c'mon, Jake, I'm serious. Olivia tells me about what her and Alura talk about. Well, most things anyway."

"Talk?"

"Well, Olivia talks, and Alura just writes things down, I guess."

"Oh."

"According to Olivia, Alura had it real hard as a child."

Jake let out a snort. "Probably no more than anybody else."

Luther shrugged. "Maybe not, but she was barely in her twenties when her mama and daddy got killed in that fire."

Jake clinched his bony fingers into two fists, and lightly pounded his knees. "I'm about tired of hearing about her poor mama and daddy. I swear, if it ain't you, it's Hawk going on about it."

Luther wondered if he should change the subject, but he pressed his luck. "What you got against Mr. Simmons, Jake?"

"Mind your own business, boy," Jake grunted at him. "And watch the road."

Luther gave him some time to cool down. "Olivia says Alura cries a lot," he announced.

Jake coughed and cleared his throat. "Yeah, when? Every time one of those visitors of hers has to leave?"

Luther's eye jumped. "Olivia says Alura misses her granddaddy."

"So what happened to him?"

"Don't know. But she says she keeps hoping he'll come back one day. Must be all the kinfolks she has left now."

Jake turned to stare out of the window—like he didn't want Luther looking at him right then. "Lot worse things than that can happen to you—like being broke and poor, spat on and cussed at because of who you are."

"Like the way you treated Hawk when he first come in the shop?" Luther kept his eyes fixed on the road.

Jake twisted his face. "Boy, seems to me you remember everything—except what's important, that is—like birthdays."

"Now, Jake, I already apologized for that. I promise I'll remember next time."

Jake snickered. "Hmph, boy, you cain't even remember your own dang fool birthday, let alone somebody else's."

Luther put up a finger. "Okay, I make you a promise: if I don't remember anything else, I'm gonna remember April fourth."

"Fifth."

"April fifth."

Jake reached for one of his stogies.

"What are you doing, Jake?"

"I'm getting ready to play the harmonica. What's it look like I'm doing?"

Luther sighed. "It looks like you trying to kill yourself."

Jake sniffed. "I ain't got to worry about that—Velma can do that just by giving me one of those looks of hers."

Luther's eye twitched and it made him nervous. "Now, Jake, I'm your friend and I wish you'd just stop smoking."

Jake gave him a look. "Okay," he said, and quietly put it back in the glove compartment.

Luther stared at him. "What do you mean, okay?"

"I said—okay, I won't smoke."

Luther swallowed. "But soon as I leave you gonna light up one anyway, right?"

Jake's green eyes twinkled dimly. "Boy, you ain't as dumb as you look."

They pulled into Luther's yard, and Luther waved to Jake as he sped off down the road. He saw Alura peeking out of her window. A big black arm grabbed her around the waist and the lights went out. Luther's stomach churned and he went into his house.

Chapter Nine

My son Tommy Lee visited Alura all the time. It was strange in a way, what with him not being able to hear, and Alura not being able to talk. But I guess they both felt they could help each other. He was tall and had big strong arms. He was self-conscious about the scar on his chin he got trying to copy me shaving myself— when he was only seven years old. My mama wouldn't let me spank him. She said he was just a baby and didn't know any better.

Olivia said she felt bad at first that Tommy Lee didn't spend more time with her. He seemed to like Alura better. But Alura was teaching him songs in sign language. He liked that. Alura trusted Tommy Lee to do a lot of things for her. She paid him to get her a tree for her, the one Christmas neither me or Luther will ever forget.

Luther said he noticed that the fella who loved having Alura's neck for dessert seemed to stay a lot longer than her other visitors. Luther kept the barber shop open that Christmas Eve. He was mighty busy because folks were getting spruced up for the holidays. Some folks told Luther he was going to go out of business if he didn't keep up with the times. But Luther insisted on giving razor shaves, unless folks requested otherwise. He said it added more of a personal touch. It was like pampering folks a little.

He had quite a few customers from out of town. Jake helped Luther out with some of them. His age slowed him down some. Luther could do four customers to Jake's one. But he felt it was just nice having Jake there. Tommy Lee was helping out—cleaning up and sweeping up hair. Sam came waltzing in that day.

"Hey, Nick, who's the new help?"

Jake ignored him. But it seemed like Sam wasn't satisfied unless Jake was riled up.

"Jake, you know how to work those gadgets of Nick's? Things have changed a lot since your day, you know."

Jake sucked his teeth as his hand gripped the comb. "I see you ain't changed, you yella-bellied snake!" he spat out, coughing. He was having trouble working the new hair cutters. "Damn!" he said. "Always changing things!" He pointed over at Luther. "A pair of good strong scissors and a sharp razor—now that's all I needed. That's the mark of a true professional."

Luther grinned, then waved to the tall black fellow who'd been sitting for a long time with his head buried in a copy of the *Casa Grande Review*. "You next."

The man had big shiny, expensive-looking gold rings on his thick fingers. There was even a big diamond sitting in one of them, and a ruby in the other. His navy blue wool suit clung to his husky body. Luther watched him reach inside the wide lapel and unbutton his jacket as he made his way to the chair. He had an arrogant dip in his stride and his shiny black leather boots clicked when he walked. He was wearing a blue and gold shirt with a silk blue tie. There was a diamond tie pin in the middle of it. He had long wavy hair that was slicked back down his head, small beady eyes set back in his head, a wide flat nose, and thin dark lips barely hiding a thick bushy mustache. There was a Kirk Douglas-chin jutting forward almost as far as his forehead. Luther could tell he wasn't from around Coolidge, or Arizona for that matter. Luther's stomach started bothering him. The man was the one who'd been staying with Alura.

The man's voice was deep and he sounded real business-like. "Light trim and a shave," he said, with a smile.

Luther noticed Jake glaring at the man, and Luther's eye started twitching. "You from around here?" Luther asked, putting a drape around the thick neck.

"Hardly. Just here for a while. I'm from Manhattan," the man boasted, turning around to flash a mouth full of baby grand piano keys. "That's upstate New York."

Luther heard Jake sucking his teeth. "Oh, New York—that's nice. Never been there. Folks say it's a sight to see."

"Yes it is. Gets hectic at times, but I *do—love—it.*"

"So why the hell you leave?" Jake muttered.

The man spun around as if someone had suddenly pulled a gun on him. He gave Jake the once-over, then rubbed his chin and smiled. "Well, if you must know, pops, I'm here on business."

The man turned around and settled back in his chair. Jake raised the cutters, but Luther grabbed his arm. Jake grunted and snatched his arm away. Bert starting putting the checkers away, and Sam went to reaching for his hat. Luther slowly combed the man's curls. The temperature was rising inside that little shop. All of the smells came to life—the ammonia on the mirrors, the shaving cream, even Jake's cigars.

"Uh, I notice you staying with Miss Simmons. She lives just across the way from me."

"Is that right?" the man said, letting out a contented sigh. "Yes, my Allie—a fine specimen of a woman," he added, carefully examining one of his diamond cuff links.

Luther nodded. His stomach started turning over. "You a relative of hers?"

The man laughed. "No—well, not yet, anyway."

Luther told me his heart leaped smack dab up in his throat. It made him cough. He started choking on his own spit. "Excuse me," he strained out, and went to the cooler for a cup of water. Luther kept his eyes on Jake. Jake had finished cutting what few hairs Doc had, but he was sure taking his sweet time putting his stuff away. Luther glanced at the clock. Twenty after five. He had to hurry.

The man seemed to be mostly aware of himself and not much else in the shop, unless it hit him right in the face. Now that *was* a thought, Luther grinned to himself. Then he sobered. He didn't know what was wrong with him. He'd never instantly disliked anybody before in his life.

"Yes, indeed," the man was saying, "fine woman like Allie belongs in a city like the Big Apple."

"And what the hell is wrong with Coolidge?" Jake snarled. "You too good to live amongst folks like us, boy?"

Jake hit a nerve. The man spun around again. There was fire in his eyes. Luther said he was praying to God that the man didn't try to hurt Jake, because then Luther would have to kill him, and he sure wasn't looking forward to it—being it was Christmas Eve.

"Now just settle down," Luther said. He glared at Jake. "Jake here don't mean no harm. That's just his way. He's right proud of this town, and he don't like folks talking against it."

The man pursed his lips and rubbed his chin. He rested his boot back on the foot support. He nodded, and his voice was slow and steady. "Only a few people I allow to call me boy: my parents and any woman so fine she can have her way every time!" He let out a bellow.

Everybody except for Jake grinned nervously. Jake grunted and grabbed his coat. "Air's getting a might thick in here," he said, ambling out the door past Sam, without looking at Luther.

The rest of the gang was heading over to Sam's Tavern. He'd spread the word that all drinks were on the house after 6:00. You're invited too, Mr. uh . . ."

"Richard Lofton," he proudly announced. "But everybody calls me Big Dick," he said winking at Sam.

"Yeah?" Sam said, with a phony grin.

Luther felt like he would throw up any minute. He glanced over at the clock. It was 5:30. His eyes shot over to the window.

There was Alura. Just like clockwork. She passed by every day, without fail at that exact time. She was all prettied up as usual. She looked in and smiled. The man saw her too. He waved for her to come in. Luther held his breath. That would have been the first time she ever set foot inside his shop. No, not now, he prayed. He couldn't bear it. More than likely the man would start mauling her again. But Alura shook her head and went on by.

"Um-um-um, fine," the visitor said. "Never talks though—just writes everything down." He let out a satisfied sigh. "But believe me, she speaks fluent body language." He turned around and flashed his toothy grin at Luther. "If you know what I mean."

Luther nodded and cut one side of his hair shorter than the other. "She ever tell you how come she don't talk?" he asked.

"No, she didn't. She's sweet, but she can be feisty at times." The man moved his hands a lot when he talked. "When I asked her why she doesn't talk, she wrote on her chalk board that it was none of my blank business. Check this, she left a blank between the 'my' and 'business,' you understand. Then she wrote at the bottom: 'I'm sure you can fill in the blank.'"

Luther snickered to himself.

The man pointed to Luther's walls full of baseball pictures. "You're a baseball fan, I see."

"Uh-huh."

"Man, the Dodgers are smoking this year."

Luther told me he envisioned the man's head accidentally catching on fire.

"Tell me something," the man said, waving his hands in the air, "who do you think will get MVP this year?"

Luther shrugged. "Hard to say."

"Well, my money's on Ted Simmons." He looked at Luther through the mirror. "You a gambling man . . . uh . . . what's that he called you?"

"Nick."

"Yeah . . . I like that . . . Nicholas."

"Not Nicholas. Just Nick. That's all."

The man laughed. "Okay, Nick-That's-All." He flashed his big teeth. "You a gambling man?"

"Nope."

"Don't talk much do you?"

"Nope."

The man nodded business like. "So, how long have you owned this place?"

Luther sighed. He didn't really feel like talking anymore. "Oh, I guess little over twenty-five years or so."

"Ever consider selling it? I can make you a deal you can't refuse."

That made Luther miss a beat in his hair cutting. He had repented for what he'd done to the man's hair earlier, so he had started to even up his hair. But now he was going to have to change it back. Luther didn't bother answering.

"Give you a real good price. Looks like you could use the money."

"Looks can be deceiving," Luther said.

The man laughed. "Well, it never hurts to ask, I always say. You might miss out on a valuable opportunity if you're afraid to take chances."

"Sometimes it's more safe to stay with what you know."

The man took out a handkerchief out of his vest and wiped his eyebrow. "That's true in a sense, but I'd have never made it to where I am if I always played it safe."

Luther grit his teeth. "Not everybody's the same," he said, turning the man away from the mirror.

"You're right there, Nick. You are definitely right there."

Luther figured it was time to stop messing up his hair and start shaving him. Folks didn't talk so much for fear of Luther nicking them. But Luther had a feeling this fella had never been taught that silence was golden.

After he started shaving him, Luther could hear things getting lively over at the Tavern. The man still talked even through the shaving cream on his face. ". . . nice little house—" he was saying. "She handmade her welcome mat . . . told her she must have known I was coming one day . . . don't know how long she's had that mat . . . really worn out—"

Luther tried to drown him out by singing Silent Night in his head.

". . . thought she was just shy, because she didn't say much, but no . . . oh man, the women in New York should be so shy!"

Luther held his breath and nicked the man's chin with the razor.

"Owww!" he screamed. "Hey, watch it!"

Luther quickly dabbed it with alcohol. Alcohol stings the best. "Sorry," he said. "Guess my mind's not on my work today. You know, with the holidays and all."

The man looked at his blood on the cotton ball and eyed Luther for a moment.

"Good thing you're my last customer," Luther said, holding his breath.

The man gave a laugh and nodded. "Yeah—good thing."

"I'll be more careful," Luther said. "I'm almost finished." He polished up his nerve and asked what he'd been dying to know. "You serious about Miss Simmons?"

The man smiled. "Serious? We're getting married. I don't think you can get more serious than that!"

Luther got rid of his razor and threw a hot towel on the man's face. Too bad scalding was the hottest he could get it. Luther grabbed the towel and swept the stray hairs off the man's back. His voice had gotten hard and crusty. "When's the wedding?" he asked.

"Oh, I'm sending for her after I tie up a few loose ends back east. Shouldn't take . . . oh, more than a week or two." He glanced at his gold watch. "Good timing, Nick, my man. I got plenty of time to have a few drinks *and* catch my plane."

Luther blinked. "You mean you not spending the holidays with her?"

The man raised his eyebrows. "No, but she understands. Real good woman, Allie." He raised his pant leg. "She bought me these boots."

Luther had had just about enough. He was ready to terminate the conversation. "That's nice," he said. "That'll be three dollars— that's for the cut and the shave."

The man eyed Luther as he took out a brown leather wallet. "Now I know why they call you Nick," he said with a grin, and planted a ten-dollar bill on the counter. "Keep the change," he said.

Luther nodded as the man strode out the door and made his way up the street toward the Tavern.

Chapter Ten

The next morning Luther was sorry he'd stayed up reminiscing the night before. After he'd come home from the shop, he couldn't help thinking about Amanda and how much he still missed her. We woke him up early, bamming like the devil on his door.

"Hey, Nick, wake up! It's Christmas!"

Luther put on his slippers, threw on his robe and peeked out the window. It was me and Olivia, Jake and Velma, Sam and Daisy, and Bert. Bert was by himself now since his wife died of a heart attack the year before. We never saw much of her anyway, so it seems like Bert was always by himself. Luther rubbed his eyes and opened the door.

"Hey, Luther," I said, "you gonna sleep all day?"

We brought in a small, bushy Christmas tree we'd cut down off the lot in Casa Grande. The smell of pine was good and strong— just what Luther needed to wake him up. Olivia and Velma came in, carrying pots and baskets. It was early, but the turkey, ham, dressing, greens, cornbread and sweet potato pie made you want to dig in right then and there. Luther said he'd go back to his diet after the holidays. Jake, Bert and Sam were lugging in bottles of liquor and boxes of ornaments. Luther was so touched I could swear he had water in his eyes.

"Merry Christmas, boy!" Jake said hoarsely, slapping him on the back. "No fun spending Christmas by yourself."

Luther noticed Jake wasn't puffing on his stogie as usual. His eyes looked more gray than green that day, and he looked kind of sweaty for it to be only seventy degrees outside. But Jake seemed in good spirits, so Luther decided not to worry. You had to hand it to Jake. Two weeks ago somebody stole his Mustang. He didn't get riled up like Luther thought he was going to, but he could tell he was disappointed. In fact, Luther seemed more upset than Jake.

Nothing lasts forever," Jake had said, and then went out and bought himself a brand new 1975 pearl white Oldsmobile with a tan interior.

When Luther thought nobody was looking, he went over to the window and glanced over at Alura's place. Her Plymouth was still there.

"I asked her to join us," Olivia whispered to him.

Luther's face flushed, and then he nodded. They both knew she wouldn't be there.

Luther said we made him feel real good that day. Everybody left around 3:30—all except for Jake.

Luther smiled at him. "This was your idea, I bet?"

Jake returned the smile. Then he did something he'd never done before. He gave Luther a hug. Luther said it almost floored him from the shock.

"Well, boy, I best be on my way."

"Wait a minute, Jake." Luther went over to the closet and took out one of the packages he'd wrapped.

Jake scrunched up his wrinkled face. "Boy, now what you done gone and done?" he asked, shaking his head.

Luther stepped back apace and struck a stiff pose with one hand in front, and held the package in back of him with the other hand like a pitcher. He bent down like he was getting ready to pitch a fast ball. "You ready?"

Jake barely bent his knees, and then cupped his hands. "Let her rip!"

Luther laughed and handled the package to him. Jake looked up at him, his eyes dimly twinkling.

"Go on, open it," Luther said.

Jake's bony fingers struggled with the package. Luther reached out to take it. "Here, Jake, let me."

Jake rubbed his age-spotted fingers. "My arthritis—guess I done too much hair cuttin' yesterday."

Luther took the wrapping off, took off the top, and handed him the box. Jake's eyes watered as he took out the monogrammed solid gold 18th century barber razor and scissors Luther had ordered four months ago. They cost a pretty penny, but Luther knew Jake was worth it.

"Look at that," Jake managed to say. "Boy, you didn't have to go and do this."

"Yeah, I know," Luther said.

Jake put his hand on Luther's shoulder. "Thank you, that's real nice. Real nice," he said, gently rubbing them. Then he carefully placed each one back in the box. He smiled at Luther. "You know, you still a darkie-lover—"

Luther nodded.

"—but you all right." Jake's voice was soft and it cracked. Those words didn't hurt Luther like they used to.

"Jake, I'm fifty-two years old. When you gonna stop calling me *boy*?" Luther hugged him.

Jake left about a quarter after four. The special Christmas service had already started. Luther high-tailed it to the bathroom to take his shower. "Darn. No towels," he muttered when he stepped out. He hadn't had a chance to do his laundry.

He went skipping over to the closet, dripping water all across the hardwood floor. Only towels left were the ones I had monogrammed for him and Amanda a long time ago. They were nice towels and they both had agreed not to use them until after the baby was born. Luther had put them up in the closet, intending never to use them. Now he was desperate.

Luther got all spruced up, shaved his whiskers and combed his hair. At his age he'd expected some bad moss up top, but it was still straight and thick looking—a kind of salt and pepper mixture.

Of course—more salt than pepper. His Sunday-go-to-meeting suit was getting a might tight in the belly, and the brown color didn't look crisp anymore. He promised himself he'd go to Yellow Front in Casa Grande the following week.

He put Alura's package in a bag. He'd gotten her a nice new Bible for Christmas. Then he jumped in his old Ford pickup and steamed down the road, his tires making tracks in the wet ground. The trees seemed to be dancing in the wind as Luther drove by. His engine was making so much noise he knew there was no way he was going to be able to sneak in. I had worked on the engine for him a few times. Told him he should just shoot the truck and put it out of its misery. But Luther had said it belonged to him and Amanda, and he wasn't ready to part with it.

Luther waved to me and took a seat in the back of the church behind Mabel and Mama. At first Luther thought something was wrong with them because they were just sitting there enjoying the Christmas program. Then the Reverend's daughter Tammy Hayes came down the aisle dressed like the Virgin Mary, and Luther just knew those tongues were going to start wagging for sure. Of course, they waited good until Tammy was well out of hearing range.

Mabel and my mama had the craziest principles. They didn't see anything wrong with gossiping about folks. They called themselves "inside reporters," but they felt it was definitely wrong for folks to *hear* you talking about them. That, according to Mama, was something you just didn't do—unless of course they did something to make her mad.

"Lawd," Mama said, "now I done seen just about everythang!"

Mabel was leaning in—didn't want to miss a word. "Mmph!" she said. That was her prompting cue.

"Talk about nerve, chile! 'Specially after what she caused to happen to poor lil' Danny—not to mention Mr. and Mrs. Simmons. You 'member, Mabel?"

"Yeah, uh-huh, I remember."

"What was it . . . eighteen . . . nineteen years ago?"

"Something like that."

"I tell you, honey, everybody knowed Tammy loved black mans. Even tried to get Hawk to play 'round with her one time."

Mabel's eyes widened. "Naw, Lue!"

"As I live and breathe."

"Now, you ain't never told me *that*." Mabel sounded insulted. "So just keep talkin'."

My mama Lucille folded her arms. They'd gotten a bit wrinkled and heavier. "I went directly to Reverend Hayes and told him: 'Now Reverend, I said, I been a God-fearin' woman all my life, but Lawd knows what I'd do if your Tammy cause my boy to get kilt like she did lil' Danny.' Told him to do something about that overgrown chile of his."

"Sho 'nuf?"

Mama nodded. "Yep. Must've done somethin' too, 'cause Hawk said she ain't never bothered him again." She let out a soft cackle. "Lawd, you shoulda seen 'Livia—mad as a cat. Wanted to scratch that chile's eyes out!"

Delores Paine spun around and shushed them. My mama didn't take kindly to folks doing that. She glared at the back of Delores' peroxide head. She'd started bleaching it ever since it started to turn gray.

Mama Lucille was raring up. "Course Tammy got it honest. Reverend Hayes may be a good preacher, but a saint he ain't!"

Mabel snickered as Delores turned again and gave Lucille a cold stare. Lucille matched her glare for glare, and kept right on talking.

"Heard the other day the Reverend been slippin' around with some old woman live over by Mr. Rawlings. Uh, you know *anythang* about that, Miss Paine?"

Delores turned fireball red. She grabbed her cane and got up in a huff. She moved over to the next aisle. Reverend Hayes glanced up at her, and Mabel and Mama almost choked themselves trying to stifle their laughter. Mama spotted Luther sitting behind them, and she patted Mabel to stop laughing.

"How you today, Mista Rawlings? Merry Christmas."

Luther smiled. "Merry Christmas, Mother Williams—Miss Mabel. I'm just fine, thank you, ladies."

Mama's eyes gleamed like a new thought came to her, and she leaned over to Mabel again. "You know Tammy Hayes done found her some new black meat, don't you?"

Mabel reared back in surprise. "Chile, who?"

"'Member that fine-looking fella from New York 'sposed to marry up with Miss Simmons?"

"Uh-uh, Lue, you lyin' for sure!"

"Mabel, I'm here to tell it. Seems he been playin' house with Miss Simmons in the day, and footsie with Miss Tammy at night."

Luther felt his stomach churning. He was ready to spit coals. He kept fidgeting in his seat, wishing services would hurry up and end.

"I feel sorry for that lil' girl," said Mabel, shaking her wig. "Finally decidin' to become a honest woman, and windin' up with a . . . a *skirt-chaser*."

Mama took a deep breath and settled back in her seat. "Well, you reap what you sow, honey, that's what I always say."

Services finally ended. Luther went and jumped in his truck and headed for home. He took out the package for Alura and stuck it in her mailbox. Then he drove his truck around the back of the house and parked it under the shed, out of the rain. As he was warming up some milk to calm his stomach, he noticed Alura driving up in her blue Plymouth. She was all dressed up, no rain-coat—but she did have on a red shawl, red boots, and carried a red umbrella.

Luther had left her mailbox open, hoping it would catch her eye. It did. She took out the package, then she looked up to see Luther peeking out at her. She waved and pointed to his porch. He waited as she lifted up her long skirt up off the ground and went into her house.

Curiously, Luther opened up his front door. There was a large package in the screen. The bow was a bit smashed, but he didn't mind. He smiled at the attached note: "Gifts, a beginning to friendship." When he opened it up he couldn't believe it. She had handmade him a small white pillow. The letters were stitched in bright red: "NICK RAWLINGS—ACE BARBER." Luther felt warm inside. He poured the milk down the drain, and turned on the television to watch the film.

Later on he wished he'd drank the milk. It stormed powerful that night. It had been raining off and on for a few days. He heard on the news that there was still a flash-flood watch in Pinal County. He'd been tossing and turning and having bad dreams that night. Three different times Alura was in some kind of trouble. She fell down a well, she was taken up by a tornado, and she was drowning in a river. Each time he arrived too late. No matter how hard he tried to save her, he just couldn't. Somebody had tied his hands behind his back. Every time he freed his hands, his feet got stuck in the mud.

He decided to get up and read for a while. He was thumbing through one of his Ellery Queen mysteries when he heard some noises out back. Delores' dog down the road started barking and carrying on. Luther didn't know if he should go check or not. Delores' soup-hound would bark if a twig broke.

He checked the clock. Twelve-thirty. His eye started twitching. He peeked outside his back window. Nothing there. Delores' dog had stopped barking. Luther put on the double lock on the door. He went to check out front. He didn't see Alura's car. He wondered where she could have gone that time of night. He kept hoping she was all right.

The phone rang. Luther nearly jumped out of his skin. He answered. It sounded like somebody was on the other line, but when Luther said "hello," the person didn't say anything. Luther said "hello" a few more times. Nothing, just a light breathing sound. Finally, there was a click and a dial tone. The same thing happened again. Luther was getting edgy. Luther kept thinking it was somebody trying to see if he was home or not. But what for? He didn't have anything folks would think was worth stealing. Then he remembered. He still had yesterday's take from the shop. Almost ninety dollars including tips. He went and checked his security box. It was still there, along with his savings bonds Jake gave him on his birthday every year, and his insurance policy.

He took out the insurance policy. It made him think about Jimmy Stewart in *It's A Wonderful Life*, the film he'd watched earlier. Maybe that's why he kept having the dreams about not being able to save Alura. He sighed. He definitely was not anybody's guardian angel.

He snuggled himself back on his couch under his blankets and dove back into the Ellery Queen book. He grunted and then skipped to the end of the book. He smiled, satisfied that the aunt had been poisoned. Her niece had switched her pills. Just as he thought. Then he dropped off to sleep.

The next day at the shop Luther's eye was not only twitching, but it was red. A lot of the fellas were hanging around the shop talking about what they all got for Christmas, and about the party over at the Tavern on Christmas Eve. Luther was barely listening. He kept wondering what Jake was up to. He hadn't seen him all day. He had decided to go visit Jake when he closed up shop.

Everybody was finally gone—all except Luther and Tommy Lee. Tommy Lee had started teaching Luther sign language, and he was catching on a little at a time. I got the news first. I came busting into the barber shop out of breath. I was so flustered, I could hardly get my words out.

"Luther . . . something awful . . . but don't panic . . ."

Luther was beside himself. He had known there was something wrong. Someone had been trying to phone him last night. "What? What?"

I tried to catch my breath. "It's Jake—he's in the hospital—in Florence!"

Luther told me that what was left of his heart, jumped down in his stomach. I could see he couldn't even think straight. He started searching for something to write on to tell Tommy Lee where he was going. But I related to Tommy Lee what was going on and asked him to lock up for Luther. He could drive Luther's truck home and we'd get it later. Luther could ride with me to the hospital. Tommy Lee nodded. Luther grabbed his hat and coat, and the Bible he always kept in the shop, and we left.

I was speeding, trying to hurry up and get there. We saw a police car behind us flashing its lights. "Damn," I said to myself. Couldn't be nobody but Charlie Parker. He'd taken over Sheriff Hickerwood's job. Charlie was always trying to show off because folks didn't give him much respect when he was a deputy. He was probably more upset because the town decided they didn't need a deputy, so he now had to do both jobs. I pulled over to the side and stopped.

"Maybe if we tell him we in a hurry, he'll let us go," Luther said.

"Don't think so. He's been looking for a chance to get something on me. Now's his chance." I sighed, reaching for my driver's license and registration papers in the glove compartment.

Charlie had a smug look on his hairy face when he came over to the car. It was cold outside. He seemed warm enough bundled up in his jacket, hat, boots and gloves. I was trying to speed things up. Soon as Charlie came over to the truck, I started shoving my license at him.

"There it is—my license, here's my registration, and I even have car insurance!"

Charlie grinned, then pushed his hat up off his square fore-head and then took off his gloves. "What you in such a hurry for, boy?" he said, chewing his gum. Then he looked over and seen Luther. "Oh, how you doing, Nick."

"Look, Charlie, I mean, Sheriff Parker," Luther said, "we just got to get to Florence. Jake's in the hospital. That's why we was speeding. We'll try to slow down."

I was just sitting there breathing hard and staring straight ahead. Charlie eyed me. "Now, Nick, I'm awful sorry to hear that about Jake. Hope he's going to be all right. But as far as slowing down, I'm afraid you weren't the one driving like a bat out of hell."

"I'll slow down!" I yelled at him. "Just let us get going!"

Charlie's eyes tightened. "Don't know if I like your attitude, Hubert Williams," he said, grinning.

Luther knew how I felt about folks calling me by my real name, and he touched my arm. When I didn't say anything, Charlie glanced quickly over the papers. He handed them back to me.

"Seeing as it's Jake you going to see, I guess I'll give you a break and let you off with a warning."

I nodded and started the engine back up.

"Oh, by the way, Hubert, how's Olivia these days?" When Charlie smiled, his teeth were as crooked as he was.

I just glared at him. Olivia had told me how he tried to flirt with her. I told her as long as Charlie don't get out of line and don't touch her, I'd let him live.

We took off again. I was going the speed limit until I saw Charlie's police car disappear in my rear view mirror. Then I speeded up and we soared down the road. The road was slippery, so I couldn't go as fast as I wanted to. But we finally got there, safe and sound.

Luther said he could smell that sickening hospital smell as soon as we came through the door. It was crowded and busy in that place. Seems around the holidays everybody gets sick, gets in a car accident or tries to commit suicide. Two ambulances were lined up at the Emergency Entrance. I don't think me or Luther noticed we were lugging mud from our boots onto the clean white hospital linoleum – that is, until the receptionist yelled at us.

"Hey, wipe your feet!" she said. "We got enough sick people here without you two tracking in more germs!"

Luther said she reminded him of Nurse Ratchet in that book, *One Flew Over The Cuckoo's Nest*. He looked down and wiped his feet. I decided to ignore her. I'd had enough of white folks ordering me around for one day.

"You got Jake Phillips here?" I asked.

She glared at me for a moment. "I'll have to check," she said, acting like she was aware of a bad smell all of a sudden.

"You do that," I told her, slow and deliberate.

We watched her run her pen down her list. "Phillips—Jake. Oh, he's in ICU. Down the hall, then turn to your left, then another right."

We found the Intensive Care Unit. Luther said the place smelled of death. He'd never known anyone to come out of there alive.

The nurse came out to talk to us. "Are you family or clergy?" she asked, matter-of-factly.

"Yes," I told her.

She stared at me, and then looked back at Luther. "Which one?" she asked.

"We're family," Luther told her.

She picked up the phone. "Yes, Dr. Callihan, there are two gentleman here to see Jake Phillips." She hesitated for a moment and looked back at us. Then she sighed. "Yes, they're family."

It seemed to take that doctor an awful long time. Luther kept fidgeting in his seat. His eye was still twitching. I nourished myself on my chocolates as we waited. Luther whispered that he hadn't been inside a hospital since Amanda was brought in—right there in the same place. They'd built on to it since then, and put in a few computer terminals.

Luther thought about the folks he'd seen leaning up against the hospital building on the way in, holding up the wall. All of them one purpose in mind—to get in a few smokes. Luther said he couldn't understand how folks could be so stupid, including me. He was so mad at Jake he didn't know what to do. He couldn't figure out what was so great about smoking. He complained that the things smelled like tar burning, they made your breath stink, and the smell got in your hair and clothes and stayed there. He said Jake's stogies didn't smell too bad, but it didn't make a difference. It had the same effect on your lungs—turned them black. His ranting and raving was enough to make me quit, for a while anyway.

Luther checked his watch. We'd been sitting there for twenty minutes. It felt more like twenty years. Olivia came down the hallway in her white cap and uniform, carrying a big aluminum food tray. She balanced it with one hand and lightly touched my hand first and then Luther's.

"Thought I'd let you two know Dr. Callihan was in surgery, but he'll be out in a few minutes."

"That's what they said twenty minutes ago," I grunted.

"What about Jake," Luther asked Olivia. He said he kept having visions of Jake's car being knocked off the road by a drunk driver or something.

"Sorry, Nick, it doesn't look good. I have to get this upstairs to a patient." Then she turned to me. "Honey, I'll be back before you leave." Then she kissed me. Luther said he felt a bit uncomfortable standing there watching us. It was the first time anybody he knew personally ever kissed in front of him.

Finally Dr. Callihan came out to talk to us. He kept looking back and forth from me to Luther. "Are you a relative?" he asked me. I nodded and then glared at him, daring him to say otherwise. He cleared his throat and turned to Luther. "I'm afraid Mr. Phillips has had a massive corollary occlusion."

I put out my hand to the doctor's stethoscope, and he flinched as if I had violated him. "In English," I told him.

The doctor shook himself as if to recover. "Mr. Phillips' lungs collapsed, and his heart . . . gave out."

Those words "gave out" kept ringing in Luther's ears. Everybody else thought Jake was stingy and selfish. But to Luther, he was always "giving out" to him. What was worse, what hit even me to the core, was when the doctor told us that because of Jake's age, surgery was an extremely high risk. "Without the surgery he's got less than a ten percent chance," the doctor said.

Luther told me those words cut through him like razor blades. Even he knew those were the worst odds you could have when it came to life and death situations. In not so many words, the doctor was telling us that Jake had played his last inning. Luther told me he couldn't imagine not having Jake around. He had everything all written down and planned out what he was going to do for Jake's birthday next year. He figured it was going to make up for all the times he forgot. No, Jake just had to make it!

Luther still had to convince Dr. Callihan into letting me go in with him to see Jake. Of course, Luther knew I was trying to be patient, because I was going in regardless of what any of the hospital staff said. The worst case would be over Dr. Callihan's dead body. Luther just told the doctor we were brothers, and me and him had different mothers. It was the truth. We were brothers in the Lord, and we most surely did have different mothers.

Luther whispered that the smell of the room reminded him of the Christmas tree we'd brought in on Christmas, but there was still that mediciny, sickly smell. We noticed a large potted plant and a vase of flowers on the table next to the bed. And there was Jake. Look like they had him plugged up with tubes everywhere he had a hole. And the tubes were hooked up to machines that were monitoring him moment by moment. Probably those tubes were the only way they could keep Jake there in the bed. He'd be out of it if he could help it.

The sight of Jake's almost lifeless body made me sink into the nearest chair. Luther hung his head and his breathing grew louder. Jake lifted his eyelids to look at Luther. I'd never seen them look so pale. Those green eyes had lost every glimmer of their shine and mystery. Jake's lips were dry and cracked. He moved his lips but no sound came out. He blinked a lot and his chest rose and fell very slowly. Luther swallowed hard. He knew what he had to do. He took out his Bible and turned to Romans, chapter 10. He looked up at Jake. I sat there with my mouth open as I watched Luther say the sinner's prayer for Jake.

"Jake, do you believe that Jesus Christ is the Son of God, that he was crucified, and shed his blood on the cross to pay for your sins, and that he rose on the third day that you can have eternal life?" Luther asked him.

Jake nodded.

"And, Jake, do you repent of all your sins and accept Jesus Christ as your personal Savior?" Luther asked.

I watched Jake nod his head and his eyes roll up. He barely lifted one of his skeleton arms. Luther grabbed his hand, holding on for dear life. Jake brought his other arm up to his chest, and struggled to make a weak smile.

He managed to make a semi-fist, and his tiny thumb pointed up. With his last breath and strength, he gave a "you're out" signal.

Luther said he felt Jake's life float out of his hand. The life sunk out of my stomach as I heard the deafening eternal beep go off on that machine. Jake never opened his eyes again.

The nurse came rushing in. She checked Jake and then ran out for the doctor. Seemed pretty silly to be rushing around now. I had to get out of there. "Luther, I'll wait for you in the truck," I told him. He nodded.

Dr. Callihan came in. He checked Jake. He looked over at Luther. "I'm sorry . . . I'm sorry."

Luther nodded and watched as they started unplugging Jake from the machines. He headed for the door. "You not out, Jake," Luther whispered to himself. "The best inning is yet to come."

Olivia said only God knows whether or not Jake made it into Heaven. Luther said that at least now Jake will know for sure.

Chapter Eleven

Reverend Hayes gave the eulogy at Jake's funeral. Sure were a lot of folks crowded together in that little church. Luther was surprised to learn that all of Jake's burial arrangements were already taken care of. He figured Velma had seen to everything, but he wished she'd consulted him about the music they were playing. It sounded like flat elevator music, mixed with a touch of slow gospel here and there. Luther said they should have played the *dut-dut-dut-tada-CHARGE!* theme like they did at the beginning of a ball game. He knew Jake would have liked that.

Luther was sitting in the back next to me. Velma was sitting up front with a lot of other womenfolk. Most of them, including Velma, were all dressed up in black with matching veil covering their faces. Jake had a habit of promising marriage, knowing full well he had no intentions of marrying anybody. Luther said they must've dyed the wedding dresses they never wore. They kept sizing each other up and giving each other mean looks, as if to say, "what you doing here?"

Luther figured they had to be women Jake had been messing around with in New Orleans, Texas and Flagstaff. Most of them young women, except for Velma. There were townsfolk who didn't even like Jake, coming in and taking a seat on the benches. The benches had gotten rickety by now and needed somebody to nail them down. Luther said he and I would volunteer. He'd started doing that a lot lately—volunteering at the church and then dragging me along with him.

Luther glanced back behind him. Mabel and Mama Lucille were looking real sad, but it sure didn't stop the comments from coming as Reverend Hayes spoke. The Reverend's voice was more shaky now, he was getting forgetful at times, and he was a lot thinner than he used to be.

"Jake Immanuel Phillips was a fine man—a pillar in this community."

"Know full well he couldn't stand Jake," my mama whispered.

"Mmph," Mabel responded.

"—lived here for over seventy years—he was loved by all—"

"Half of New Orleans, look like," Mama commented.

"Um-hum. Robbin' the cradle," Mabel said. "Girl, wondered what he promised 'em. Um-hmph."

Mama Lucille nodded her all-white head up toward Velma. "Chile, probably same thang he promised her. And look at that veil. Best beauty aide she ever invested in."

Mabel shook her short wavy wig and giggled.

"She been trying for years to get 'im to marry up with her," Lucille added.

"Now, Lue, tell me something I don't know."

My mama's voice got even softer. Luther had to strain to hear what she was saying. "Course I got news for all of 'em. Ain't a one of 'em gettin' a dime."

Mabel gave her a surprised look and then she covered her mouth. "Oh, that's right. Gul, it's been so long, I almost forgot . . ."

Lucille patted Mabel. "Well, chile, sit still—'cause they all's in for a big surprise."

A stunned hush, murmurs and whispers bounced off the walls of the church as Alura entered in a long-flowing olive green dress with long sleeves. Her hair was all pinned up on top of her head, and there was a hint of baby powder as she passed by. Luther turned to look at me. I kept looking straight ahead, putting on my best poker face.

Velma went to huffing and puffing and looking around indignant like when Alura quietly and delicately walked up front. Alura's arm was holding her black shawl wrapped around her shoulder. I heard Luther swallowing hard. We watched as Alura looked expressionless down at Velma.

"Excuse me," Alura said, "I'd like to sit down please."

Luther said he couldn't believe his ears. Alura was actually speaking. Her voice reminded him of honey dripping from a honeycomb. He felt his heart shift gears and his thoughts raced a mile a minute. Alura looked up over at Luther and nodded. That was the first time Luther had been that close to her. It was then he noticed them: those almond-shaped green eyes!

Reverend Hayes cleared his throat, glanced around the church like he wished he was any place but there.

"Yes, we will miss Jake Phillips . . ." More sweat beaded up on his bald head. ". . . but the Lord found it in his heart to leave part of him with us . . ." Reverend Hayes wiped his head with a handkerchief. He finally realized there was no way he was going to get around it. "Jake Phillips is survived by his . . . lovely . . . granddaughter—Miss Alura Jacqueline Simmons." He then nodded to Alura and held his breath.

I wish I had a penny for every gasp, moan and groan in that room that day. They had to use a ton of smelling salts to revive Velma. Me and Luther were Jake's two pallbearers. Sam, Bert, Tommy Lee and Isaiah Taylor were holding onto the sides and back. When we got up to lift the casket, Alura looked up at Luther again. He saw the sadness in those eyes, but there was no doubt about it: she was Jake's kin all right. The temples of her hair were a little salt and pepper color. Her rosebud mouth was surrounded by what was definitely Jake's high cheekbones.

As we were riding over to the grave site just outside of Coolidge, Luther told me he had already decided to take a few weeks vacation. He figured he'd spend some time fishing up at Coolidge Dam. He was sure gonna miss Jake. Jake was the only one who

Luther thought remembered his birthday, besides Amanda. I always remembered Luther's birthday, but it made me feel uneasy, buying gifts for men. Luther said he understood.

It was important to Jake, though—that kind of stuff. He'd do the same thing to Luther every year. February twelfth would roll around and, as usual, Luther wouldn't pay it any mind. Jake would wait good until either Luther was getting ready to close up shop, or he'd come over to Luther's house and sit with him for a while, having a drink or a smoke. Luther would be staring at him, wondering why he was hanging around so long. He enjoyed Jake's company, but Luther was a morning person and needed his sleep.

Finally, Jake would start to leave, then turn around, pull out an envelope from his pocket, flash that wide smile—his green eyes twinkling—and say "Happy Birthday, boy!" Then he'd give Luther a five-hundred-dollar savings bond. But Jake was gone now, and Luther suddenly felt very old.

Velma was bawling like the devil at the grave site. Luther said he knew it wasn't so much she would miss Jake as she knew she wouldn't be getting all of his money. Luther shook his head at the thought. Alura was gonna be awfully wealthy. Luther thought that maybe now she wouldn't carry on with any more men.

It was still drizzly outside and the tree leaves, turning yellow now, were rustling past us. You could smell liver and onions coming from the cafe down the street. Luther watched Alura when they were putting Jake in the ground. Olivia and the rest of us were standing there with tissues, sniffing and moaning. I wasn't crying—it was just raindrops—made it look like I was crying. I did sniff a few times—cold going around. Mama Lucille and Mabel weren't crying but they were real quiet. Alura didn't shed a tear—in front of us, that is.

After they put Jake's body in the ground, Olivia whispered something to Alura. Alura hugged her and shook her head as if to say "no." Luther wanted to say something to her too, anything to comfort her, but she really didn't look like she needed any comforting. He said she reminded him of his mama. And, probably just like his mama, Luther thought, she'll probably go home and cry herself to sleep.

Alura went to her car. That's what was missing, Luther realized. There was no hearse. Just as well. Jake had said it was just "putting on airs" to be riding around in a limousine in Coolidge. Luther hurried over and opened the door for Alura. She smiled.

"Thank you," she whispered to him, and started up the engine. "I guess I'll see you tomorrow," she told him before she drove off. It was more a statement that a question.

Luther opened his mouth to tell her he wasn't going to be at the shop tomorrow if she was planning on passing by, but she sped off down the road.

It was a real puzzle to all of us, why Alura had started speaking again. Most folks thought it was something to do with Jake. Maybe she hadn't wanted to get talking to him. But she sure could talk well now, just like she'd never stopped.

Luther got up early the next morning. The rain was gone. The air was clean and fresh. He could almost taste the bass cooking on the skillet. He could hardly wait. He had packed his camping stuff last evening. He was just loading his fishing poles when the phone rang.

"Hello," Luther said, impatiently. He was sure somebody was gonna try to sell him something again.

"Uh yes, Mr. Luther Rawlings, please." It sounded like a man, but he had one of those sissy-like voices, Luther thought.

"Speaking."

"Mr. Rawlings, this is David Harper. I'm with Harper, Sells and Rowan."

Luther giggled a little. It sounded like a comedy team.

"We were appointed administrators for the estate of Jake Phillips. We'd like you to come into our offices today to discuss his will."

Luther's eye twitched. "Well, I was just on my way out . . ."

David Harper let out a high-pitched "Oh?" Then he cleared his throat. "Yes, well, I apologize for the late notice, but we're working on Jake Phillip's schedule."

"Schedule?" Luther almost snarled. "Jake don't have no schedule. He's dead."

There was a silence for a moment. "No, Mr. Rawlings, you don't understand. We're working with a time frame previously *arranged* by Mr. Phillips."

Luther sighed as he envisioned other folks catching all the fish. "Okay, tell me where and what time, but you got to give me plenty of time to get there. My truck don't run like it used to."

There was a short laugh, then, "Well, Mr. Rawlings, after today it's possible you won't have that problem again. Now, we're located at—"

"Wait a minute, I got to get a pencil," Luther said. He put down the phone and went to the kitchen drawer. He pulled back the curtains and looked outside. Alura's car was gone. He came back with a pencil and a scratch pad.

"Okay, I'm back."

"Yes, it's East Camelback Road." He gave the number. "Suite 208—we're on the second floor."

Luther stopped writing. "Camelback? Why there's not . . . oh, now don't tell me you in Phoenix?"

"That's right."

Luther shook his head. "That's going to take too long. I'll never get to go fishing on time. I don't like fishing at night by myself. Besides, my truck's not running that good, like I said."

David Harper's voice grew louder and higher. He was sounding impatient. "Mr. Rawlings, don't you realize that Jake Phillips was a wealthy man? And he's named *you* in his will?"

Luther didn't like the way he emphasized "you" as if to imply Luther wasn't worthy or something. "Can't you just mail me whatever it is he left me?"

David Harper sighed, then he talked a lot slower, but he was still loud. "Mr. Rawlings, it doesn't work that way. By law we are required to do this in person—if at all possible!"

"Well, now I done already told you, I don't have a way there. So if you going to be that way about it, you can just keep the money. It's not going to bring Jake back no way!"

With that, Luther slammed down the phone. He was still muttering to himself when he drove off. "Smart aleck, young fella. Should've asked to speak to Mr. Sells or Rowing. Money should go to Alura, anyhow. Jake don't owe me a thing."

As Luther was heading down the road, he kept wishing Jake was alive and sitting next to him. Last time he and Jake went fishing was about a year ago. They had a bet on who would catch the most fish. Luther beat Jake five to his one. Jake promised he'd beat him the next time.

Luther cut his trip short. He told me he kept thinking about Jake and why he had to fool everybody about Alura being his granddaughter. Luther felt Jake could have trusted him. It wouldn't have mattered, Luther thought. When he got home, me and Olivia were waiting for him.

"What you two doing here?" Luther asked, surprised to see us. "You take off work out of respect for Jake, too?"

I smiled. "Naw, Luther, today's a holiday." I helped him bring in the rest of the stuff out of his truck.

"Oh," Luther said. "Well, somebody could have reminded me. I could've used some fishing company."

"Me and Olivia got to spend some time by ourselves," I told him.

Luther put his poles and tackle box in the storage closet. "So, as I said, what you doing here?"

"Alura sent us to get you," Olivia told him.

Luther stopped. "Oh, that's right. They're reading Jake's will."

"She said you didn't have a way to get there," I told him. "They were supposed to start at nine, but Alura refused to let them start without you."

Luther looked at the clock. "That was what, four hours ago."

"Yeah, I know," I told him.

Luther took off his fishing hat. We waited another half hour while he showered and changed his clothes. Finally, he put on his Sunday-go-to-meeting hat.

"Well, I guess I'm ready."

"Are you sure?" I said. "Maybe you want to read a novel or something before we leave."

Olivia hit at me. "Stop it, Hawk."

Luther grinned. "Come to think of it—"

I grabbed his arm. "Oh, no you don't. Let's go."

It was a nice drive to Phoenix. We listened to the radio on the way. I sure hated going by that sewage place off I-17.

"Whew, Luther—that you?" I said, holding my nose.

Olivia laughed. "Hawk, cut that out!" she said, punching me in my arm.

"I was just sitting here wondering when you were gonna excuse yourself," Luther laughed.

I remembered Tommy Lee telling me how Luther needed to improve the shop. "Luther, what you gonna do if Jake's left you any money?"

Luther was quiet. Of course, none of us knew what Jake had done in his will, but it was a sure bet he'd have seen Luther all right. I knew Luther would rather have Jake back instead. "Seems to me like it's awful soon for them to be doing this. Of course, I know it's not Alura's doing."

I was snacking on a chocolate bar. "They said that's the way Jake specified it in his will. Alura felt same as you, but Jake already arranged everything before he died."

Luther sat there twirling his hat, trying to get up the nerve to ask us what he'd been dying to know. "How long you two been knowing about Jake's secret?"

Olivia looked over at me and nudged me to answer. She looked down at her hands.

I swallowed and shrugged. "Been knowing all my life. Willie told me."

Luther stared at me. He was feeling uneasy, but he had to ask. "How come . . . you know, why . . . ?"

"You mean how come he didn't want to be black?" I blurted out. Luther nodded and looked away. I threw the wrapper out the window.

"Hawk!" Olivia scolded me, pointing to the unlawful to litter sign.

I nodded like I always do, knowing full well I was gonna probably do the same thing again. Still don't understand how she put up with me.

"Can't say as I blame him," I told Luther. "Not that I'm condoning what he did. But you know how things are. It took me a long time to figure it out. Jake didn't kill my daddy, but he knew who did. My daddy hated Jake's guts for what he was doing, but he kept his secret. If they didn't have nothing else in common, they had that." I could tell Luther knew I was talking not just about Willie—but about me. "Maybe Jake felt he'd have never gotten anywhere in life if he'd have told the truth."

Luther pursed his lips. "But what about Mr. Simmons? He was a smart lawyer."

I glanced over at him. "Yeah, so smart he got himself and his wife killed."

Olivia struck a thoughtful pose and turned to Luther. "It's pretty hard growing up when you're too white to be black and, well . . . too black to be white. You know what I mean? I guess Jake just took whatever road he thought was easiest."

Luther sighed. "Maybe, but Jake said times were changing—and they are. We even saw a interracial couple out here last year. And I'm sure there's others."

"That's right," I added. "But folks' attitudes just ain't changed that much. They still full of prejudice like they always were. They just know how to hide it better now."

Luther's voice was almost a whisper. "Is that what you think I do—just hide it?"

I snickered. "If you do, Luther, you doing one heck of a job!"

"Of course not, Luther," Olivia told him. "You're probably one in a million . . . but just look what they did to Martin Luther King and . . . there's too many to count."

Luther looked at me. "But didn't they say he was shot by a black man?"

I nodded. "Let's just say, it wasn't *who* killed him so much as *what* killed him."

Luther was quiet for a while until we got off the freeway. I turned off the heater.

"Well, how you two feel about it?" Luther asked.

"What's that?" I said.

Luther didn't look up. "About black folks and white folks—together?"

Olivia looked over at me and smiled. "You mean dating and getting married and stuff?" I said.

"Yeah."

I laughed. "Well, thanks anyway, Luther, but I already got Olivia."

Olivia hit at me. "Hawk—behave."

Luther smiled. "Sorry to disappoint you, Hawk, but you definitely not my type either."

I pretended to cry. "Aw, now you gone and hurt my feelings. Luther, I really thought you cared."

Both Olivia and Luther were laughing with me. Luther had finally relaxed.

As we rolled up in front of the high silver-glassed building, we tried to catch our breath. Luther noticed Alura's Plymouth and several other cars in the lot. We went through the door to the lobby. A young white man with a crew cut, dressed in a security guard uniform, had us sign in. He then pointed us to the elevator. And there it was, Luther told me later. That sad elevator music. The elevator reminded him of a coffin. He thought about Jake.

When we got off the elevator, we found a door with brass knobs and the words *Law Offices of Harper, Sells, and Rowan* across the front.

"You two go in. I have to find a bathroom," Luther said.

"Don't fall in now," I called to him. He waved me away. "Come on," I told Olivia.

After winding around a few hallways, Luther finally found the men's room. When he got back to the law office, he took off his hat and opened the door. He found ten eyeballs staring back at him. It was cold inside the office and it smelled like jasmine. Alura smiled and Luther nodded at her.

"Afternoon," Luther said.

David Harper stood up. He was in his late thirties. Luther told me later that Harper reminded him of a blond-haired Liberace. He could tell Harper didn't think too much of him, no matter how nice he was being to him. Olivia and I sat quietly.

David Harper shook hands with Luther and offered him some tea. Luther's eyebrows narrowed. "No, thank you," he said.

"Well, as you probably know—I'm David Harper, attorney at law."

Luther nodded.

David Harper motioned to another gentleman next to him who was leaning back in a Victorian chair. "This is my partner, Lyle Rowan."

One of the man's hands was cupped to his hairy chin, his elbow resting just on a big shiny wood desk and his legs crossed. Luther nodded and extended his hand. The man nodded but didn't make an attempt to shake hands. Luther cleared his throat and took the empty seat in the semicircle. Luther reckoned he probably had an attitude problem because his name was last on the door.

"Please, have some tea," David Harper offered again. Luther shook his head. He noticed I didn't have any either. In fact, nobody was drinking any except Mr. Harper and Mr. Rowan.

Mr. Harper got underway with the meeting. He did most of the talking. Mr. Rowan changed positions every once in a while and kept looking at his watch. I could see he was making Luther nervous. Luther seemed glad when Mr. Rowan excused himself and left, saying he had another appointment.

It turned out Jake left me and Olivia one of the houses down the street from where Mr. and Mrs. Beaumont, Amanda's parents, used to live—plus ten thousand dollars to put in a trust fund for Tommy Lee's college education! I couldn't believe it!

Jake left everything else to Alura: mortgages on homes, stocks and bonds, other real estate. Mr. Harper also said something about money market accounts and whatnots. He said Jake's total assets was $800,000! Luther said he was so happy for us and for Alura. He knew Jake had money, but he had no idea how much. Alura was calm the whole time, as if none of it surprised her. She just sat there and nodded as Mr. Harper talked.

Finally, she asked "Did my grandfather say anything else, Mr. Harper?"

"No, Miss Simmons—that was all. Oh, but he did leave you this letter."

Mr. Harper took out a long white envelope out of a cash deposit box and handed it to Alura. She reached for it with one dainty white-gloved hand. Her charm bracelet tinkled.

"Thank you," she told him.

I was wondering about Luther. It didn't seem like he was going to get anything after all. "What about Luther?" I finally asked.

"Oh yes . . . I almost forgot," Mr. Harper said, with a grin. He had big pearly white teeth. Luther said later he had the feeling Mr. Harper forgot on purpose.

"Mr. Rawlings, I apologize for making you go through all this trouble."

We all stared at him. He took out a small package from the deposit box. You could tell he was not enthusiastic and obviously knew nothing about what all this meant to Luther—or maybe he just didn't care. Seems like the exciting part was over for him. He read from his legal document again.

"'And to my best buddy, Luther—AKA Nick—AKA boy—AKA you know what—gotcha—I leave: one, this 1916 autographed baseball by Babe Ruth when he and the Boston Red Sox defeated the Brooklyn Dodgers to win the 1916 World Series.'"

Mr. Harper picked up the baseball as if to show them and then yawned. "Oh, excuse me—it's been an awfully long day. Now, let's see . . ." He went back to reading. "'And, two, my favorite diamond-studded watch.' He also left you this letter." He handed the watch and envelope to Luther. "Oh, Mr. Rawlings," he said, remembering, "I should mention—and I'm sure you'll probably be just as confused as I am . . . I don't know why, but Mr. Phillips insisted on letting the watch run down and setting it for an exact time. I'm not sure . . ." He put down the paper and inched his shoulders up, looking at Luther for an answer.

Luther slowly opened the letter and read it to himself. He recognized Jake's handwriting. It was worse than his own. "Guess what, Luther? The game starts at two. Gotcha again! Your friend and pal, Jake." Luther looked at the watch. It was set for 2:30. Luther snickered and shook his head. Then he started laughing until tears came out. Mr. Harper stared at him like he'd gone mad, but Alura just smiled, along with us.

Mr. Harper appeared a bit uneasy at that point. "Well, I guess that about wraps it up," he said, almost hopping to his feet. "My office will be contacting you for any last minute paperwork."

We got up to leave. Mr. Harper turned to Luther. "I apologize, Mr. Rawlings. Mr. Phillips had insisted that the will not be read unless you were present. I had no idea . . ."

Luther cradled the box to his chest. "Mr. Harper—and you can tell Mr. Sells and Mr. Rowan for me—Jake already gave me more than I'll need while he was alive." Luther cupped the ball to his chest and his voice cracked. "This is the best present I ever got in my whole life." Luther shook his hand. "I wouldn't have missed this for anything in the world." He smiled and nodded to Alura.

Outside, Olivia and Alura locked arms as they went to the car, like girls sharing a secret. Luther kept wondering what they were whispering and giggling about. Probably more "girl stuff," he told me. He gave me a hug. "Congratulations, Hawk, when you gonna move?"

I grinned. I hadn't told him yet. "Soon as me and Olivia get hitched."

"You mean you asked her already?"

I gave him a look. "Are you kidding? I asked her a few years ago! She told me we'd get married soon as we could afford a house." I grinned and held up the papers. "And here it is."

Luther said he was pleased. "That's right fine, Hawk. I'm happy for you." There was some sadness in his voice though as he watched Olivia saying "see you later" to Alura.

"Course, you know I can't get married lest I have one more thing . . ."

"I thought you had what all you needed."

I put my hand on Luther's shoulder. "Well, I got to have my best man."

Luther looked at me and his face turned red. "You serious?"

"Serious as a heart attack—uh, yeah, Luther, I'm real serious."

"But what about Isaiah? He's more than a friend. He's your cousin, for goodness sake. How's he going to feel?"

I'd already worked it out with my cousin Isaiah. I grinned at Luther. "Olivia still got an extra spot on her list for a bridesmaid."

Luther laughed and then looked at me. "Now, you sure about this?"

I nodded and unlocked the doors. Luther plopped his hat on his head. "Then I guess I'll meet you at the church house."

It was good to hear Luther laughing again.

Chapter Twelve

A lot of things happened a few years after that. Sam closed down The Tavern after he and Daisy moved up to Washington. Folks started going to Casa Grande and Phoenix for night life. Some of them went up to San Diego and Vegas for the weekend. Didn't see much of Bert except once in a while. He took a lot of ribbing about Jake being his best buddy and Jake being a black man.

Look like a getting-married epidemic struck Pinal County. Luther said he never saw so many people rushing to the church to get married—mostly young ones. And of course that led to a lot of pregnant women. Luther reckoned it was like the chicken and the egg: you didn't really know which came first—that is, until later. Because even though Mabel or Mama Lucille never finished high school, both of them were real good at calculating what they called "baby making dates." They even shortened it to "BMD" just so most folks wouldn't know what they were talking about. It took me and Luther a few Sundays to finally learn their system. They subtracted the Marriage Date (MRD) from the Baby Born Date (BBD) and that gave them the Baby Making Date (BMD). Now, if the BMD was less than eight or nine, that meant (according to Mama) "somebody been squeezin' the juice out of the orange 'fore it got picked off the tree."

Mabel wasn't as fast as Mama when it came to calculating. Mama would be leaning in next to Mabel when folks came into church, and whisper, "Now thas' a six . . . thas' a seven . . . and Lawd, would you believe thas' a three?"

"Shameful, Lue," Mabel would comment, and then they both would almost hurt themselves trying to stifle their laughter.

Even Delores Paine finally hooked the Reverend Hayes whose wife passed away two years prior. But Alura hadn't gotten married yet—even with all those fellas she'd been with. Luther said he was glad folks finally settled down about Jake. He said it finally made sense when he found out Jake was Mrs. Simmons' daddy. Alura owned the bank now, and the mortgages on most of the homes in Coolidge and other places. Folks were nervous—thought she might retaliate on them for all the gossiping and meddling, and especially for what happened to her mama and daddy. But she didn't change a thing—except to hire Olivia to work for her.

Olivia said Alura was thinking of opening up a beauty shop. I told Luther I hoped it was far and away from the barber shop. He just shook his head, but I knew he was hoping they set up shop close by. Tommy Lee started cutting hair in Luther's shop, and he set him up in a booth like Jake had done for him. Luther had gotten better at signing. He was whipping words off faster with his fingers than Delores Paine could talk. Now you know that was fast!

Tommy Lee gave Luther some ideas on how to improve the shop. He told Luther it was time to change with the times. It would increase business. Luther said he thought business was doing just fine, but he told Tommy Lee he liked his ambition. Luther was planning on early retirement in three years anyway. He told Tommy Lee he could take over then and run it like he wanted to. Tommy Lee got so excited, instead of signing he grabbed Luther and hugged him.

Luther said it was at me and Olivia's wedding that he noticed just how much of a man Tommy Lee really was. Mabel was the Matron of Honor. I thought she was too old, but Olivia insisted. Alura and Olivia's four half-sisters were the five bridesmaids. Gladys, who played the piano at church, said she would be glad to play for us. There she was missing a beat as usual. Then there was my best man, Luther. I could tell he was feeling uncomfortable.

Gladys, Reverend Hayes, Delores and Luther were the only white faces in the crowd. My mama Lucille, other relatives, Mabel's friends, Mabel's relatives, and Olivia's friends from the hospital were there.

In fact, most of the black folks still alive in Coolidge were there. I should have listened to Olivia who said we should have gotten an exact count of the number of guests. We almost ran out of food and it was crowded inside the VFW, but Alura was paying for everything. I wasn't going to complain.

I had some of those sugarless chocolates wrapped inside my pocket that I wanted to snack on real bad. I'd finally given up smoking for good. And, of course, I put on a few pounds. I kept trying to time when I could eat one, but somebody was either staring at me or nodding at me, making me even more nervous. I noticed Luther tried not to look at Alura too hard. She came down the aisle arm-in-arm with Isaiah Taylor. Mama had made all of the wedding dresses. The place was full of amber-colored chiffon material and lace and whatnot everywhere. Mama would yell at me when I accidentally stepped on something. But she sat smiling in her amber-colored brimmed hat on my side of the wedding party. Strange how Mabel sat on Olivia's side. I say strange because that was the first time I ever saw Mabel and my mama Lucille sitting apart. I guess me and Olivia's wedding was one day they wouldn't be thinking of gossiping. I even saw Mama looking at folks like she dared them to say anything negative.

Then the music changed. Everybody turned their heads. I stuffed a piece of chocolate in my mouth. I almost choked. Olivia came down the aisle. It liked to knocked my socks off! Luther told her later how beautiful she was. Alura must've straightened out Olivia's hair. Luther said he never knew it was so long. It hung down to her round shoulders. Mama had made a white dress that came just below her knees. It had long sleeves and a high collar with lace stitched in pretty designs.

I could tell she was nervous too because she was shaking in her heels as she walked. Tommy Lee was towering over Olivia as she held onto his thick arms. I noticed my mama, and Mabel and some of the other women were applying the tissues they'd been holding onto, as if they were just waiting for the time when they'd be using them.

Later, Olivia urged Luther to ask Alura to dance. But some other guys beat him to it. In fact, whenever he got close to Alura, they'd give him a look like they dared him to speak to her.

So he just went over and got some punch instead. He told me that even though he was supposed to be the best man, he sure didn't feel like it.

So, after all the dancing and opening up gifts, and cutting cake, and shoving in me and Olivia's face, we were off to New Orleans for the Mardi Gras. Alura gave us tickets for wedding presents. Luther gave Olivia a book of Emily Dickinson poems and a crystal vase. He gave me a certificate for a whole year of free hair cutting, and a large box of miniature Snicker bars. I realized at that point that somebody stole my idea.

Luther said he enjoyed the wedding, but he was glad when the ceremony was over. He had fumbled around for the ring. He reckoned he just knew folks were whispering to themselves about how come he was best man instead of Isaiah. He told me he kept thinking about how he hadn't given Amanda a big church wedding like he knew she wanted. I know that Luther started missing her again that day.

Alura left, and Luther was not too far behind her. He drove slower than she did. He got home and went in the house and hurried up and took off his suit. He could hardly breathe. He sat down in Amanda's favorite chair and read Friday's mail. There was a thank you note from Alura. He couldn't understand why it took her so long to thank him for the Bible he gave her the Christmas Jake died. Luther figured she probably had so many other people to send thank you's to. He felt he was probably last on the list.

He noticed Alura didn't have any more men callers after she got Jake's money, but he still worried about her. It'd been several years since that Richard Lofton from Manhattan was supposed to send for her like he said. Luther was glad he hadn't—he didn't like him anyway. Still, he wondered what happened to him. Luther got his answer a few months later at the department store in Casa Grande.

He rode up there one Saturday evening to stock up on supplies. He liked Shopes, but they didn't sell stuff in bulk. Plus, Shopes was under new management. Hattie's Smart Mart didn't have everything Shopes had, but it did have a large quantity cheaper, of the stuff Luther mostly used in the barber shop. Tommy Lee told him he'd save more money up at Hattie's.

Luther noticed Hattie's big grin as soon as she saw him coming through the door. He knew she just had the lowdown on something good.

"Hey, Nick. Haven't seen you in a while," she said, pushing her toothpick to one side.

"I know," Luther said, taking off his hat. He put on his glasses and then took his list out of his pocket.

Hattie smiled. "Specs, Nick?"

"Just for reading." Luther grabbed a basket and headed for alcohol and shaving cream.

Hattie was waiting on the only other two customers in the store, but she kept glancing over at Luther as if she couldn't wait for him to hurry up.

"Thank you, come again," Hattie told an elderly gentlemen who'd just bought a case of Rolaids.

She called over to Luther. "Finding everything all right, Nick?"

Luther waved as if to say "yeah."

Finally, Luther pushed his basket up to the counter.

"Where you been hiding yourself?" Hattie asked, checking the price and ringing it up on the register. "Thought you'd given up coming here."

Luther shrugged and shook his head, looking at the batteries. "Nope, just been shopping in town mostly."

Hattie looked up at Luther. "Hard to forget about what happened to Jake. Just terrible!"

Luther sighed. "Yeah, I miss him. Wow, Hattie, seems like your prices go up every few months."

Hattie smiled and her voice got low, even though nobody else was in there. "Is it true? I mean, about Jake being a nig—I mean black?"

Luther had known Hattie a long time, but if looks could kill, she would have dropped dead right then and there. He shot her a look more penetrating than a bullet from that .22 Jake used to tote around.

"Jake was Jake!" Luther snarled at her. "Always will be to me." He took out his wallet even though Hattie was still ringing up his order.

She seemed to hurry up after that. "Sorry, Nick. I guess you and him was friends and all . . ." She bagged up his order, and another wicked smile appeared on her face. "Shameful about that city fella his granddaughter was gonna marry."

Luther was shifting his weight back and forth impatiently. He stopped. "What about him?"

Hattie bagged up the last of Luther's order. "Haven't you heard? He run off with no other than Tammy Hayes." Hattie giggled. "I swear, I don't know how the Reverend Hayes can hold his head up in public these days."

"When was this?" Luther asked, peering at her, trying to detect a lie.

Hattie took out her toothpick. "Now, Nick, you know I'm not one to gossip—but, it couldn't have been no more than, what, three and a half months ago. I know it's true, because I used to see them sneaking into the Casa Grande Motel a few times. Shocked me, it did." Hattie picked her gold tooth. "That'll be sixty-nine dollars and forty-eight cents."

Luther was mad. "That for the supplies—" he shoved three twenties and a ten at her, "—or the gossip?" he growled, and then he left.

Luther knew Hattie must've been right. It was about that time he noticed Alura stopped taking care of herself like she used to. She didn't pin her hair up any more. It just flopped down her back and shoulders, looking like it hadn't seen a comb in a day or two. Luther wanted to talk to her real bad, but he didn't. It didn't stop her from passing by though.

Bert shook his head. "You think with all that money she'd take care of herself better."

"Guess she not feeling too well," I said. "Olivia thinks the shock of Jake's death just kicked in."

Luther said I must've been right, but he felt it was more than that. Deep down he couldn't help but feel guilty. Alura had given Tommy Lee a note inviting Luther over for dinner two months ago. He didn't show up. He said he could've kicked himself for being a fool. He just sent a note with his apologies by Tommy Lee, but he never told Alura the real reason he didn't come.

Alura's dinner invitation had been for that following Friday evening. But Luther had already planned to go to the Barber Convention that weekend in Tucson. Luther said he didn't know whether or not that Richard Lofton fella was coming back for Alura at that time, but eventually he decided that dinner with Alura would be a whole lot better than shooting the breeze with a group of strangers who looked like they didn't know the first thing about barbering—because not many of them had much hair!

Even though Luther had already paid his money and they said he couldn't get it back, he had decided he would call Alura and accept. But that very day Sam, who'd kept The Tavern, showed up from Washington for a visit—unannounced. The checkers and dominoes had gone from the corner now, but he didn't seem to mind. Guess he hadn't come to play games.

Sam had done real good up in Washington. He said things were a whole lot different up north in the cold. He talked more sophisticated, and seemed to lose his "r's" when he talked, but he seemed at first to be the same old Sam.

Luther and he reminisced about the good old days for a while. Funny, Luther said, neither one of them brought up Jake. Luther wanted to ask him how come he didn't come to the funeral, but he guessed he already knew the answer.

Sam told him he flew into town for an important meeting with a group he called "The Brotherhood." Sam kept saying it was the answer to all the world's problems. He said The Brotherhood had been around a long time and was "grossly misunderstood." He said the meeting was the next evening at eight o'clock, and that Luther was getting a personal invitation. Sam stressed that it was a low profile group, and he shouldn't mention it to anybody.

Luther was real curious by then, especially when Sam said it was a Christian society and dedicated to world peace and harmony.

"How far is the meeting?" Luther asked him.

"Not too far out of town," Sam said.

That was all Luther needed to here. He went.

Sam offered to drive the both of them, but Luther wasn't planning on staying too long—just long enough to satisfy his curiosity and donate a few dollars to their cause. So he got into his old truck and followed Sam—all the way to Mesa. Luther's truck stalled a few times and it sounded real bad. He kept mumbling Sam's name every time he had to stop.

"Mesa! That's what he called not far out of town!" He started to turn back a few times, but decided to keep going since Sam waited for him each time. Luther figured that was the least he could do.

Luther followed him to a large church building. They had arrived late so it took Luther at least five minutes just to find a parking spot. He found one almost two blocks down. He noticed

Sam had his own personal parking spot inside the lot. Luther had never seen so many Mercedes, BMWs and Cadillacs in one spot, except in the car dealership. It didn't look like they needed any donations.

Sam was looking at his watch as Luther trudged down the block up to him. "Come on. They've already started."

Luther noticed two police cars at the door. He figured they needed them in case somebody tried to steal one of those fancy new cars. Luther was startled. He recognized one of the policemen. It was Charlie Parker. He'd quit after Jake died. Never said where he was going. Luther knew I was one person who didn't cry when Charlie Parker left. Luther started to speak to him, but Charlie pretended not to know him.

Luther could hear cheering and shouting coming from inside as they approached the first set of double doors. He usually felt good about being in church, but not that evening. And his eye twitched.

When they opened the doors, he noticed a large crowd. The men were wearing black business suits and they were on their feet yelling and waving in agreement to the man standing on the stage speaking into a microphone. Luther said he kept hoping Reverend Hayes didn't get any ideas about a microphone. He told me that was all we needed—to be able to hear the Reverend better—our life-long dream.

Some men greeted them with a handshake and a smile to Luther.

"Good evening, brother. Good to see you."

He handed Luther a visitor card and then ushered them to two empty seats on the middle row toward the back.

"Damn," Sam muttered. "I wanted to sit closer."

Luther gave him a look like he should repent—foul words in the Lord's house, but Sam didn't, so Luther let it roll off. He glanced around for the bathroom. He was hoping he could leave out the back when it got close to nine. But thirty-five to forty minutes was all Luther could stand. He couldn't believe what he heard.

They were going to create world peace and harmony by getting rid of what they called "the troublemakers" who "have polluted and soiled this wonderful country." They said the troublemakers included the Blacks, Mexicans, Indians, Orientals, Jews, foreigners, and "sexual deviates." Luther figured they were talking about homosexuals. They said all that kind should be wiped off the face of the earth.

Well, enough was enough. Luther had to use the bathroom real bad, but he decided that place wasn't worth using the toilet in. He didn't even try to leave quietly. He tripped over somebody's foot making his way out. He was going to apologize until he turned around so he could look the man dead in the face. His head was gray now and he was carrying baggage under his eyes and chin, but Luther never forgot a face. It was Freddie Hooper from his sixth-grade class. Luther had heard he joined the Air Force. Freddie's little brother got killed in the Vietnam War. Luther thought he'd left Arizona and moved to Atlanta.

Then Luther noticed something else. One of Freddie's arms was missing. At first Luther thought Freddie didn't recognize him, but when their eyes met, Freddie raised his finger in recognition. He fixed his mouth as if he was going to say something, and then must've changed his mind when he saw the rest of them staring at him. At that point it didn't matter to Luther. He was out of there.

He didn't reach the end of the block good where his truck was, before he heard Sam coming up behind him, out of breath.

"Nick! Wait up!" Sam never could run too fast when he was young. He had to be about seventy now. He caught up with Luther and grabbed his arm. "Nick, where are you going? The best part is coming."

Luther couldn't even look at him. "I'm going home."

"What's the matter?" Sam asked. "Just give it some time."

"Sam," Luther said, shaking his head. "That's not what I call a brotherhood. That's the KKK!"

Sam was still catching his breath. "Okay, I know what you're thinking: white sheets, hoods, crosses burning, hangings—right?"

Luther nodded and stared at him. "The thought had crossed my mind, yeah."

Sam put his hand on Luther's shoulder. "Now see, that's what you don't understand. They don't do that any more. Didn't you listen in there?"

Luther took out his keys and pursed his lips. "Sam, I listened real good. White supremacy. You all just as bad as the Black Panthers. Only you using the Bible to justify your hate and killing. My Bible don't say one word about one race of people being better than another. And it don't say anything about getting rid of folks because they are different. Jesus said we're supposed to love people who are different from us. And if they're unbelievers, we're supposed to love them enough to help them give up their sins and accept Christ. That's what I always thought, anyway. In fact, Jesus was about as different as different could get."

Sam shook his head. "Nick, you've got to hear the whole thing first. Then you can make up your mind."

Luther snatched his arm away. "I heard enough."

With that, he opened the door and got in the truck and closed the door.

"Look," Sam said through the open window, trying to persuade Luther. "I know Brother Zack gets carried away sometimes—but when he talks about getting rid of folks—"

Luther put his key in and started up the engine. "You mean the troublemakers."

"—he's talking about being separated."

"You mean, let Blacks be with their own kind?"

"It's the same for all of the others, too. It confuses people and causes problems when you try to mix, especially when it was never meant to be!"

What Sam said next cut to Luther's heart. "Look what happened to Jake! He didn't know whether to be Black or be White. He spent his entire life living a lie." Then Sam pushed the knife in deeper and turned it. "And his poor granddaughter Alura—and her mother—living their entire lives, Nick, separated from Jake because he didn't want his secret to get out. " Sam's voice lowered and was more steady. "Nick, we say nobody should have to live that way."

Luther sighed. He shifted gears and Sam stepped away. Luther left without waving goodbye. He didn't know how long it took him to get home. It didn't matter. He didn't sleep that night anyway. Even the warm milk didn't put him under. He didn't bother telling anybody he wasn't going to be at the shop the next day. Tommy Lee had a key and he could take care of everything.

Luther stayed inside hibernating. He unplugged the phone and watched TV most of the day. After a while, he went down to the cellar. He found some old scrap books of his mama's. He hadn't really looked through them all, even though he'd been saving them for years and years. Luther had a hard time throwing things away. Seems like everything ended up having some kind of value.

He glanced through his mama's certificates and awards she'd gotten for her painting when she was in school. She only went to the sixth grade. Luther found some of his baby pictures. He was dressed in a long gown. He shook his head and smiled. Also inside a box was a diary. Luther debated a few moments whether or not he should read it. He felt guilty at first, but his mama was gone. It'd been way too many years.

His mama was a woman of very few words. Looked like the diary was a daily account of one year: 1923. His mama was about seventeen years old then. The man she described in her diary seemed somehow familiar to Luther. He had jilted her. In fact, she found out he was already married to somebody else. She had been so hurt. It wasn't until a few months later, she discovered she was pregnant.

Then she talked about another man who came on the scene. She loved him too. The second man loved her and wanted to marry her, but she knew she couldn't. She didn't want to use him. She was trying to decide what to name the baby. She admired Martin Luther because of his work during the Reformation. She was going to name him Luther. But what about a middle name? She decided to name him after his daddy. "Bernie won't mind," she wrote. "He don't even know Luther exists." Then Luther remembered. Bernie VanHorn in Las Vegas!

And that's the day he learned who his daddy was, there in that cellar. It all made sense when he remembered how well VanHorn has treated him and Amanda.

Luther could've fallen through the ceiling when several pages on his mama wrote:

"Wish I could marry Jake, but folks would never approve. Jake told me his secret. I'd be so afraid Luther would find out one day. I do love Jake, but I just can't do it! I'm not that strong, I guess. He's so successful and he is handsome. I'm sure he'll find somebody else to marry. He'll probably forget all about me one day. I just wish . . ."

Luther's mind was racing when he came out of the cellar. His eyes, feet and back hurt, and he felt very old and tired.

Chapter Thirteen

Luther tried his best to avoid Alura, even though he still worried about her. He couldn't avoid the fact that his eye kept twitching. A few of the folks were still preparing for the Parada del Sol up in Scottsdale. Luther said it was silly to give a parade for the sun with the weather like it was. It had to be one of the coldest Februarys Coolidge had ever seen. The rain made it worse. Luther was used to it raining during the Monsoon, but the weather was warmer then and his joints didn't ache so much. He wished he'd stayed home rather than opening up shop. Me and Tommy Lee were both home with the flu that day.

The weatherman on TV had said a storm was coming. Who knew, he was gonna be right for a change! Luther could hear the drumming sound of those hard pellets on the barber shop rooftop. He could handle that, but bright streaks of lightning came with it from time to time. He could barely concentrate on what Bert was saying. He watched the empty streets outside. That big palm tree in front of Bert's drugstore was doubled over in pain, its huge leaves trying to cover its face. Coolidge, just like most of Arizona, wasn't prepared for flash floods. The streets didn't have very good drain systems, so there were large ponds on each side of the road.

Luther peered out at the police car's red, yellow and blue sparkling lights. It was Eddie Hickerwood, the new Sheriff. Eddie had gone against his own convictions from a long time ago. His family had wanted him to be sheriff like his daddy—just not crooked like him—but Eddie had said he was going to medical school. Folks said he flunked out at college and took an office job for the County.

Eddie looked every bit like Sheriff Hickerwood, but he was a whole lot nicer and helpful. Eddie's car was parked behind Vanessa Stewart's green Dodge. It was stalled again. Luther sighed. He'd heard talk about them dating. Funny, he thought, how Eddie was the usher at church and Vanessa sang in the choir when they were little, but they couldn't even sit together at one time. Eddie's parents and Vanessa's daddy had passed away—the only people who objected openly to blacks and whites dating in their family. Everybody else—you knew how they felt by what they didn't say. Luther figured Eddie was Sheriff, so why should he really care—but most of us knew they weren't ready to come out in the open for sake of Eddie's career goals. He talked now about being Governor one day.

Luther waved to one of the Taylor twins who was closing up the Trading Post. They looked so much alike, Luther didn't know if it was Clinton or Vinton. The boys had to be in their twenties now. Luther watched the twin hugging himself, rain poured onto his baseball cap that was turned backwards on his oversized head. He jumped on his motorcycle. His engine roared as he sped away shaking his head, as if to say, "how come it's so cold?"

Luther took in a deep breath as he flipped out the light switch on the barber pole outside. In this weather, he was sure nobody else was getting a haircut or shave today. He glanced at the big wall clock that me and the fellas at the shop gave him a few years ago to celebrate the fiftieth anniversary of the first barber shop in Coolidge. Each hour of the day was supposed to represent an inning, plus three extra. The man who sold it to Olivia at the hospital had smiled and said, "We always assume there's a tie in the bottom of the ninth." On the half hour, instead of chimes, the *dut-dut-dut-tada-CHARGE!* song would blast loud and clear. Each hour the *Take Me Out To The Ball Game* song played cheerfully. Five more minutes before the ball game song was supposed to play. Luther clicked off the *on* and *off* switch that controlled the songs. Thank goodness it had one, Bert had said. It didn't bother Luther. Drove some of us crazy if we stayed too long in the shop.

"You might want to turn up the heat a bit," Bert said. Luther saw him rubbing his knuckles. He had his head buried as usual in the classifieds of the Arizona Republic. He said he was thinking about moving to Sun City.

Luther watched Bert stretched out across that old vinyl sofa. It was in pretty good shape since Luther just took the plastic off seven months before. He had to. Everybody was complaining about how the heat made the plastic stick to them. They had to peel their clothes off it just to get up. Bert had complained the most. Luther said he should have been pretty happy now.

Luther took off his apron and laid it up on the counter next to the cash register.

Bert pushed his square bifocals up on his long nose. "What's that gal building over there, Nick?"

Luther's eye twitched. "Who?"

Bert looked up exasperated. "You know. Alura Simmons."

"I don't know," Luther said, counting the day's take. "Why?"

Bert folded his paper. "Well, earlier today she come in looking real bad," he said, shaking his head. "She bought a hammer, some nails, a hook, the thickest rope I had, and some candles too, I believe." Then Bert shrugged. "Shucks, I told her she looked like she was getting ready to hang somebody!"

Luther's eye twitched and his stomach pinched inside.

Bert stretched. "They say, hell hath no fury like a female scorned. Heck, that city fella better not ever show up again."

Luther's mind was racing, when Olivia bammed on the door. He hurried to the door and let her in. She raced in and put down her umbrella.

"Here," Olivia said, handing a damp envelope to Luther. Her voice had a mixture of concern and mystery. "Alura gave me this earlier. She told me not to give it to you until 5:30 today," she said pointing to the clock. Then she put her hand to her chest. "I swear I almost forgot! See you later." She ran out and jumped in her new Volkswagen.

Luther tore into that letter. He recognized Alura's handwriting.

Dearest Nick:

An imprisoned heart without a key,
An endless love, but not for me;
Love came again and left once more,
Makes me wonder what I'm living for.
One special time you sent your care,
But a loveless life I cannot bear.

Love Forever,
Alura J. Simmons.

Luther's hands started shaking and his eye twitched even more. He had to rub it. A hook, a rope. A loveless life she couldn't bear. "Oh God, oh God, oh God—no!" was all he could get out.

"What's the matter?" Bert asked, jumping to his feet.

Luther stared at him, but didn't see him. "Lock up for me, Bert. I got to go!"

Luther grabbed his raincoat and hat and shot out of that shop. His boots sloshed in the mud as he ran out to his truck. He jumped in and turned the key. Lord, it stalled on him. And it was so cold outside. Luther had forgotten his gloves, and his hands were aching. He was getting frantic and kept stomping on the pedal. "Come on!" he pleaded. "Please, God, please!"

Luther looked up and saw Bert staring at him through the window and rubbing his age-spotted, nearly bald head. It seemed like forever, but finally that old engine turned over. Luther put on his wipers and steamed down the muddy road. He was barreling down that road like lightning. He kept praying all the while. He thought about his mama. He thought about Jake. Seemed like everything he loved ended up leaving him one way or another. He was three-fourths of the way there. The engine cut off and died.

He had been meaning to buy a new truck like I told him he should, but he said him and Amanda had their first date in that truck. It was special. Amanda was gone, and Luther cursed himself for not being able to let go of her memory. He cursed himself for letting other folks' attitudes rule his life. He also cursed himself for being afraid to do what God had put on his heart to do.

Well, he finally realized there wasn't any more life going to come back into that engine, so he got out and started running the best he could down that muddy road. He wasn't as spry as he used to be, so he fell down a few times. He got right back up, though. Olivia had told him he needed to start jogging for health reasons. She was getting her wish now.

Luther's hands and raincoat were filled with mud. He was getting tired and weary, and he was breathing pretty hard. He slowed down to a fast walk. Then his knee started cramping. It hurt like the devil. Lord, it was so cold out there! Something was definitely wrong, Luther thought. It wasn't supposed to be that cold.

He limped over to a fence to catch his breath. It used to be Mr. and Mrs. Beaumont's, Amanda's parents', old house—only it was fixed up now. Luther remembered that was where they had planned their first date. As he looked up and wiped his tired eyes, he could have sworn he seen Jake grinning at him! He blinked his eyes.

Luther wasn't too far away now. He could see Alura's house down the road. It looked dark, but he could see a glimpse of a shadow. He mustered up all the energy he could, huffing and puffing. He finally made it. When he got to the gate, there were no lights on, but he could see a candle flickering in the window. The curtains were closed, and he didn't see any sign of Alura. He ran up to her porch, tracking mud all the way. That was the first time he'd ever set foot on her welcome mat. After all those years that thing was shot to hell—all dirty and trampled on, strings coming out. He couldn't even make out the letters.

As a force of habit, and without really thinking about it, Luther wiped his feet on the mat. His heart was beating faster than the electric drums they have nowadays. His hands were numb, and he rubbed them on the side of his coat. He could barely smell somebody cooking something. He hadn't eaten, but food was the last thing on his mind. He tried his best to catch his breath and he felt a little dizzy. He started coughing.

Luther didn't know if he should charge in or what. Praying to the Lord, he knocked heavily. His fingers were aching. Nobody answered. He knocked again. This time harder. He pounded on the door. Still no answer. "Miss Simmons! Alura!" he yelled.

No signs of life. He could just envision charging in and finding Alura's small, delicate body hanging lifelessly by a rope. Lord, please don't let that be the case, he prayed.

He tried the knob. His heart skipped a beat when he found the door was unlocked. Something inside him dreaded opening up that door, scared to death what he might find. His eye hadn't stopped twitching all that time. He still felt dizzy, but he steadied himself and swallowed. Slowly, he pushed open the door, holding his breath. He stepped in. Lord, what he saw!

Alura was sitting at one end of her dining table. Her hair all done up on top of her head, and her face—prettied up like it once was. There was a place setting for two. Fine china. A red rose inside a small crystal vase was set at one end of the table, and a big candle inside a copper candleholder was glowing on the ceiling. In the center of the table was a great big white cake with a picture of a red and white barber pole, and a baseball bat and ball. And in letters printed in red icing were the words, *HAPPY BIRTHDAY NICK.* Alura stared up at him, those green almond-shaped eyes twinkling in the candlelight. Then she flashed Jake's wide smile— minus the tobacco stains, that is.

Luther said he stood there shocked in his muddy boots—his mouth hung open. All kinds of mixed emotions swelling up inside of him. The one he'd been holding back the longest, got through first. He tried his best to warn his eye ducts, but the tears burst through against his will. They streamed down his weather-beaten cheeks. Alura got up. She had on a long-sleeved blue denim dress and boots. She went over to a desk and pulled out several tissue. She went over and delicately wiped his face. His body seemed to warm up just by her slight touch.

"Guess I must look a sight," he said, taking the tissue and wiping his face, putting mud all over his red cheeks.

Alura smiled. "I'll get you some towels so you can clean up."

Luther nodded. He watched her disappear gracefully into the back room. It was nice and warm in there. He noticed her taste in furniture was more modern than his. It was decorated in black and lavender lacquer. Alura liked collecting miniature replicas of everything. She had several bookcases of such things throughout her house. There was a small baby grand piano in the next room— black with a lavender vase and white rose setting on it.

After Luther washed up, he spent one of the best nights he'd had in more years than he would care to admit. He was nervous at first. He couldn't eat much of the dinner Alura had cooked. But after a while he felt right at home. Alura had a calming and patient nature about her. They both sat on the sofa reading through some of the award-winning poems Alura had written.

"You liked to scared me to death," Luther told her later.

Alura blushed a little and smiled. "Well, it seemed the only way I could get you to visit me. I really do apologize, though."

Luther shook his head. "Oh no, don't be sorry. If anybody should be apologizing, it ought to be me." He wondered if he should tell her the real reason he didn't show up that time for dinner.

"Do you want some more coffee?" Alura asked him.

"No thanks. That was plenty. Cake was real good. I like coconut." He stopped and turned to her. "Can I ask you something?"

Alura leaned back against the sofa. "Sure, Nick, ask me anything you like."

"The hook and the rope, and the poem? Was Bert and Olivia in on this?" he asked. She smiled. Then Luther looked like he had a thought. "I bet I know," he said, pointing his finger, "It was Hawk!"

Alura smiled and her green eyes twinkled. She handed Luther one of her family albums and moved closer. He could smell baby powder. She pointed to each picture, explaining to Luther who they were and how they were related to Jake. He loved listening to her soft voice.

Then she looked at Luther. "You still miss him, don't you?"

"What, miss Jake?" Luther said. "He's not one codger you soon forget."

Alura laughed. "That's for sure. My dad always said that Jake and I were a lot alike—stubborn as mules."

Luther cocked his head to one side. It was hard for him to picture Alura with a stubborn will. He cleared his throat and dared to ask. "How do you feel about what Jake did?"

Alura's eyes went to her hands. "You mean passing for a white man."

"Yeah," Luther said, not looking at her.

She sighed and picked up the dishes and carried them into the kitchen.

"Can I help you?" Luther asked.

"No, it's okay."

When she came back in, Luther was going to take back his question, but she answered anyway.

"I don't have anything against white people, Nick—or anybody else for that matter . . . but a person should be proud of who they are."

They both looked at each other for a moment and were quiet. Alura went over to the bookcase and picked up the miniature rocking chair. "Do you know how it felt to go all those years not being able to sit on his lap and talk to him, or even hug him in public because somebody might find out? For a long time I hated him for that." Her voice cracked on the word "hated." She set the rocking chair back on the case and sat in the easy chair across from Luther.

"And mother—her heart broken when he didn't approve of her marriage to dad." Luther could see tears forming in her eyes. "Do you realize that he didn't even come to their funeral after the fire?" She put her face in her hands. "He had no right! He had no right to do that to us!"

Luther was nervous, but he went over and bent down on one knee next to her chair. He took out his handkerchief and put it up to her hands. She looked at him and took it. She sniffed and tried to gather herself together.

"I'm sorry . . . I'm spoiling your birthday," she said, dabbing it under her eyes.

"No, you're not," Luther said. "But we can't be crying and carrying on. Shoot, it's wet enough outside."

Alura let out a laugh and gently touched his arm as if to say thank you. She was so beautiful and tender, Luther thought. How could those fellas leave after knowing her? He couldn't understand it. He thought about that Richard Lofton fella. It was beyond him how they would let somebody like that run loose. Luther figured he had to be out of his mind: running off with Tammy Hayes when he could've had Alura.

A million thoughts must've run through Luther's head at one time before he finally decided that if she wasn't going to let him kiss her, she would have moved away from him—because she was real close to his face. He moved in closer to the pitcher's mound. He wound up. He sent his slow pitch. She tilted her head and closed her eyes. For a minute Luther thought it was a little outside. Nope—right on target—straight across the plate. Her lips were soft and smooth.

When he pulled away she slowly opened her eyes and smiled. Then Luther got up and sat back on the sofa and put his hands on his knees. He knew his batter was up, but he wasn't ready for no foul innings. And he sure wasn't about to send in no pinch hitters. He figured Alura had more than her share of those kinds of players.

She got up and moved to the window. "Nick, there's something I have to tell you . . ."

"Okay," Luther said.

"And, please, Nick . . . try to understand . . . I know it took me a while . . ."

Luther kept staring at her, wondering what she was talking about.

She turned to him. "I'm not sure how you're going to feel about this . . . well, Granddad's gone now . . ."

"What's the matter?"

"Remember when they found Sheriff Hickerwood in Prescott? He'd been hung?"

Luther nodded. "Yeah, I remember. He committed suicide."

Alura sighed. "No . . . I'm afraid he didn't . . ." She rubbed her cheek on the curtain. "Granddad paid some men to kill him." She looked away.

Luther's mouth and eyes widened in unison. "Jake?" he said, in disbelief.

Alura nodded. "I had my suspicions when it happened, but they were confirmed after Granddad died. He confessed everything to me in a letter he left with the lawyer." She went over and sat next to Luther. "Nick, please don't let it change the way you feel about him. You see, Granddad never forgave Sheriff Hickerwood for what happened to my parents."

Luther's mind was spinning. "You mean Sheriff Hickerwood had Mr. and Mr. Simmons killed?" He remembered what Jake said about a lot getting by him.

Alura shook her head. "I really don't know. But in Granddad's letter he said he held Sheriff Hickerwood responsible. He said that if Sheriff Hickerwood didn't do it, he knew who did and was covering it up. To Granddad, that was the same as being guilty. He said in his letter that he may have hated the black blood in his veins, but he still believed in what he called 'skin for skin'." She touched Luther's arm. "Please, whatever you do, don't you hate him."

Luther sighed. "Hate Jake? Don't think I could ever do that. I don't agree with what he did . . . in fact, I'm glad he never told me. Don't know how I would've dealt with it, but . . . no, Alura, I could never hate Jake." Then he checked his watch.

Alura got up. "I know—you're going to have to leave—probably have to open up the barber shop early."

Luther got up, too. "Well, can I help you clean up?"

"No, but thank you, anyway," she said, going to the closet to get his coat. "I can handle it." She sounded like she would cry again.

Luther noticed she had a dishwasher—something he didn't have. She followed him to the door. He plucked his hat off the rack. It was almost dry. He took his time putting on both his coat and his hat, trying to stall for time. He turned to her.

"I really do thank you for this. I really did enjoy myself. Everything was really nice. Really."

Alura's smile was weak but at least it was there. "And you're really welcomed, Nick," she said. "You really are."

They both giggled. Something told Luther to ask her while she was laughing. He looked down at the ground. "You know, I'd feel mighty honored if you'd accompany me to church this Sunday."

Alura sighed and seemed nervous. "Well . . . thanks, Nick, but I—"

"You don't have to stay long," Luther said. "Service starts at nine and it's over at eleven. Sometimes Reverend Eddings—that's the new assistant pastor—gets long-winded, but all we have to do is look at our watch a few times, fidget in our seats a might, cough a few times and start looking at the door, and he wraps his sermon up real quick after that.

Alura shook her head and smiled. "You are too much." Then she looked at him. "Seriously—tell me—you really enjoy church, don't you?"

Luther twirled his hat. "Yeah, as a matter of fact I really do. In fact, I've been considering . . . oh, never mind, now don't go trying to change the subject on me like Jake—" Alura smiled. "What do you say, Alura? We got a real choir now. Olivia sings in it. I bet you sing like an angel?"

"Yeah, and I bet you preach like Saint Paul," she kidded him. Luther gave her a look. She grinned. "Almost thou persuadest me to be a Christian." Luther was surprised. She'd been reading the Bible he gave her that Christmas when that Richard Lofton fella was *visiting* her. "Nick, please don't take this the wrong way . . . I don't really know a lot about God. I don't even know if I believe he exists . . . but I refuse to be a hypocrite. I won't pretend like I'm holier than thou, when it's just not true."

Luther shifted his weight. His voice was softer. "Is that what you think of me? That I'm some kind of hypocrite?"

She touched his arm. "You, Nick? Oh no—never." She walked over to the fireplace and picked up the miniature doll house replica. "You know, my mother took me to church when I was a little girl. I remember sitting there listening to the pastor ranting and raving about Hell and how we'd burn throughout eternity in fire and brimstone. Well, it frightened the hell out of me—so to speak. I thought to myself: I know I don't want to go to that awful place. The pastor said we should 'get saved' and then we'd go to Heaven. The opposite of Hell. He described it as a place where we'd live throughout eternity, that is, we'd live 'happily ever after'."

Luther just stood there.

Alura turned and faced him. "And it was all a lie, Nick—every word of it. Just look at the world around us—all the killings and wars. Oh, let's not forget the hatred. Just because people have a different color of skin or even different texture of hair. Or maybe because this one is wealthier, this one's poorer, this one has greater abilities or talents than someone else—or maybe not. It all makes me sick!"

She came back over to Luther. Her voice was a mixture of crying and laughter. "And do you want to know the worst part? Listen to this! They do it all in the name of guess who? God! Some of them truly believe they're doing God a service. And God lets them do it. So he must approve of it." She opened the front door. "So, no, Nick, I'm sorry. If those are the kinds of people who will be in Heaven . . . well, you can count me out."

Luther took a deep breath. He was beginning to see Jake in her more and more. He gently closed the door. "Can I say something?"

"Of course."

"I respect your feelings. And I know you went to college and probably a whole lot smarter than me . . . but, Alura—please—whatever you do, don't blame God. He gives folks, what you might call, a free will. He wants you to love him, but he's not going to *make* folks love him—or even make them do the right thing, for that matter. You've got to stop closing off your heart to him—and let him in. He's not going to hurt you, because he . . . because he loves you . . . he really loves you."

She was real close to Luther so he cleared his throat and took a step back. "Besides, think about the hard job he's got. Believe it or not, he created Delores Paine. Go figure that one, why don't you. Now how'd you like to be in God's shoes and have to take the blame for that?"

Alura released herself in a laugh. She hit at Luther in a playful manner and shook her head.

Luther put a hand to her cheek and she grew real still. His face was serious. "Let me tell you a little story and then I'll go on home."

She didn't say anything, but she was listening.

"There's these two rooms. You come to the first room and there's this big sign on it reading *Hell*. You walk in and there's a huge banquet table. It's got all the best foods on it—fit for a king—all tasty and delicious—make your mouth water. But something's wrong. All the folks sitting around the table are crying, complaining, arguing, and some of them are near about ready to starve to death!"

Alura's mouth was parted, hanging on his every word.

"Now when you look real close you see the reason why. Not one of these folks has any arms. All they got to use is these real long sticks coming out of the socket of their shoulders. And every time they reach out, grab the food and bring it over their heads to feed themselves—the darn food falls to the ground. And they barely, if ever, get a bite to eat. Now I don't know about you, but I get awful cranky when I'm hungry."

Alura smiled, her hands clasped together.

Luther went on. "Then you come to the other room. The sign on this one says *Heaven*. In here you got the same identical thing. Table set same exact way. All the best tasty food, make your mouth water just smelling it. But something is just a might different in here. All the folks are laughing, talking and having the best time you ever did want to see. I mean they are eating and just as full as they wanna be. Not one tear in the bunch."

He noticed Alura eyes getting watery. Inside, he knew. He went on. "Now these folks got long sticks instead of arms, too." He lowered his voice and spoke slow and steady. He didn't want her to miss his point, so he demonstrated with his arms held out straight. "But the difference is, each of these folks are picking up the food, reaching over, and feeding the person who is sitting directly across from them."

He gently took her hands. "You see, Alura, I don't care what anybody else has told you, but it's not so much what church you going to that counts. It's not even so much what the other people there say or do. It's who *you* are and who *you* become when you're there. That's what I believe God looks for." With that, he kissed her on her cheek. "Good night," he said.

After Alura closed the door, Luther remembered that his truck was stalled way down the road. He decided not to bother Alura. Besides, it had stopped raining. He sloshed on home, seeing as his truck had finally "given up the ghost." Alura had told him Bert was in on the plan, so he didn't worry about him or the shop. Bert had a key and had closed up for him once before. Luther figured it was the least Bert could do, especially after fooling him. But then, he did have a good time.

Chapter Fourteen

Luther stayed around the house most of the weekend—fixing the leak in the roof, cleaning, doing his laundry. He'd pushed his truck over to the side of the road out of the way and left it there. He noticed Alura was gone all day Saturday. It had stopped storming, the flash flood warning was over, but it kept drizzling off and on. It cleared up by Saturday evening. Me and Olivia found out Sunday morning that Luther had been trying to reach us—just as we thought he would. We deliberately didn't answer the phone when it did ring, but anyway we were gone most of the weekend. Had something special to do.

Sunday morning Luther woke up with the sunlight streaming through the curtain. He rolled out of bed. He had mixed emotions. This was a special day at church for him, but he wished he'd gotten in touch with Olivia to see if she would have talked Alura into going. And he wished he'd gotten in touch with me so I could tow his truck for him. So, when the phone rang that Sunday morning, I knew it was Luther.

"Hello?" Olivia answered. She sounded groggy.

"Morning, Olivia. Luther. Is Hawk around?"

Olivia blinked at the clock next to the bed. "Now, Nick Rawlings, where else would my husband be at 6:30 in the morning?"

"Well, can I speak to him?"

All Luther heard was a lot of whispering. I got on the phone.

"Hey, Luther, what you doing up so early? Church don't start for a while yet."

Luther sounded anxious. "Need your help. My truck give out on me. I need you to help me fix it—you know, maybe later on this evening—or first thing Monday."

"So, how you getting to church?"

"Why else do you think I'm calling?" Luther said, noticing Alura's car was still gone.

Luther heard us whispering again. "We'll be over to pick you up about 8:30," I told him.

"I'll be ready. Oh, by the way, where's the best place—"

I'd hung up the phone by then. Luther told me later that he decided right then and there to go truck hunting on Monday. He needed something more reliable. Last time we all were at the movie, we stopped by the Toyota dealer in Casa Grande. Luther had talked about how much he like the 4x4. I told him I wouldn't mind having one myself. Olivia had just shook her head with a "men and their toys" look on her face.

Luther started his shower to running and took another look outside toward Alura's place. Still gone. He guessed she thought he'd be bugging her about going to church if she stayed home. After his shower he got dressed, had a cup of black coffee and a piece of toast. He didn't have much of an appetite. He sat and read the paper until he heard us blowing the horn. He knew it didn't sound like my truck, but he figured who else could it be? He gulped down the rest of the coffee, threw on his coat, grabbed his hat and Bible, and headed out the door.

Luther couldn't believe his age-old eyes! I grinned when Luther saw the Toyota truck. Now he knew where we'd been all weekend. Luther wasn't too happy that we hadn't told him. He was even more upset that we bought a blue one like he said he was gonna get. He felt we were just rubbing salt in his wounds. He didn't expect something like that of me, but Luther knew money sometimes changes folks. I could tell he was determined to put up a good front. It was the Lord's Day, but Luther felt like it wasn't his. In fact, he pretended not to notice.

"Good morning," he said, opening the door and getting in next to Olivia. It was a much tighter squeeze than my truck. "How you doing?"

I smiled heartily. "A whole lot better now that I'm woke up."

"Morning, Nick," Olivia almost sang. "Nice day, don't you think? Oh, I love it after it rains."

"Uh huh," was all Luther said.

After we headed into town, I peeked over at him. "Well, Luther?"

"Well, what?"

"What do you think?"

"About what?"

I grinned. "About the truck. Rides real nice, don't it?"

Luther shrugged. "Guess so." He was looking straight ahead.

"Like the color?" I asked him.

Luther shot me a hot look, but caught himself. He sighed and then nodded. I saw we were about a half a mile from the church. I pulled over to the side of the road.

Luther looked over at me. "What's the matter? We gonna be late."

"You drive," I told him. "I want you to see how a real truck is supposed to feel."

I got out, and Luther, mumbling under his breath, got out and came over to the driver's side. I looked at Olivia and she giggled. Luther thought she was making fun of him. He was mad at both of us. But Luther knew I was bigger than him and could whip him if I wanted to. Guess that was the only incentive Luther had for holding his temper.

Luther took off down the road and we sat with him, watching. After a while he said he was feeling guilty about being so selfish. I figured he would after he drove it. He stopped at the light just before we were gonna turn into the church.

I grinned at him. "Stops on a dime, don't it?"

Luther sat there, probably wishing my mouth would stop on a dime. But he forced a smile. "Yeah, sure does. You got a real good truck, Hawk. Couldn't have picked a better one myself." There was a bit of sarcasm in his voice. I pretended not to notice.

He pulled into the church parking lot. Mama Lucille and Mabel and some of the other folks greeted him with smiles.

"Mornin' everybody," Mama beamed at us.

I gave her a kiss on the cheek. Olivia grabbed Mabel around the waist, which was even harder to do these days.

Mama grinned over at Luther who was parking the truck. "Morning, Mr. Rawlings," she called to him. "How you like the truck?"

"It's nice." Luther looked like he just knew all of them were gonna rub it in. It didn't matter, he decided. It was still a special day for him. He shrugged. He just wished Alura had come. He made sure the windows were rolled up and he locked the door. Then he noticed that the truck had steel-rimmed tires. They were sharp. I handed him his hat and his Bible. Luther handed the keys to me, but I didn't take them.

I waved my hand. "Sorry, Luther, those don't belong to me."

"What?" Luther said. He thought I was crazy. He just knew I didn't go steal somebody's truck.

We all stood there grinning at him.

"Now?" Olivia asked me.

"Yeah, now."

Olivia took out an envelope and handed it to Luther. He scrunched up his face. "Now what?" He opened it up.

"To our good friend, Luther, AKA Nick. Ride in style. Happy Birthday. Love, Olivia, Hawk and Alura."

Luther stood there dumbfounded.

"Close your mouth before something fly in," I told him, giving him a gentle slap on the back.

Olivia hugged him and Luther squeezed her in return. He turned to me. Then he threw his arms around me. Luther shook his head and his eyes watered. "I don't know what to . . ."

I gave him a wink. "Just say thank you, and let's go get to service. You gonna have plenty of time to brag about your truck later."

Luther laughed. "Thank you. Oh, my . . . thank you." He looked around. Still no Alura, but in some ways, he told me later, he felt she was there.

"Alura paid the most," Olivia whispered to Luther. "Sorry she couldn't be here, but you know how she feels."

Luther nodded. Inside, he hoped we were playing another trick. Maybe Alura was in the church waiting. He was wrong. Luther loved his birthday presents, but the one he wanted most looked like he wasn't going to get. How was he ever gonna get Alura to the altar for a church wedding if he couldn't even get her to come to Sunday service!

He sat next to me and Olivia. My mama and Mabel were in front of us. Reverend Hayes was sitting in the center seat in the pulpit. Church had just started, and already he looked like he was ready to fall asleep. We had gone through the formal part of service when I saw Luther rubbing his hands together like he was nervous. Reverend Hayes stood up.

"God is so good to us, brothers and sisters. He keeps sending us workers for his vineyard." Both he and Reverend Eddings moved to the aisle. Reverend Hayes motioned to Luther. "Would you please come up front, Brother Luther Rawlings."

It was me and Olivia's turn to be surprised this time. Luther walked up front, his hat and Bible in his hands. Luther was trying his best to make it through this.

"Praise God. Today Brother Rawlings has accepted the calling the Lord has put on his life." With that, Reverend Hayes unfolded a long, black polyester cloth like the one Reverend Eddings wore around his neck. Luther had his head hung down and his hands and hat behind his back, standing stiff as a board. Reverend Hayes went through his prayers and asked Luther a lot of questions—most of which he'd better have said "yes" to. It was like swearing somebody into office. Finally, Reverend Hayes put the cloth around Luther's neck. He smiled at Luther and motioned for him to turn around and face the congregation. "Sisters and Brothers, please pray for and encourage our new Reverend, Luther Bernard Rawlings."

"Bernawrd?" one of the Taylor's grandchildren called out, and the children started snickering. Some of the grown folks, too. Even Luther smiled.

"That's Reverend Bernard," Reverend Eddings said.

"A-MAN" the congregation yelled out. Then Reverend Hayes motioned for Luther to take a seat in the pulpit. I was so proud of Luther sitting up there. I could tell Olivia was too. She was all smiles.

"I'm sure glad the Lord called you and not me," I ended up telling Luther later on.

"You probably wouldn't have been home, anyway," he said, smiling.

It was almost time for Reverend Eddings to bring his message. Luther wouldn't get to speak until a month later. Reverend Hayes motioned for the choir to sing. That's when Mama Lucille and Mabel got started. I heard most of what they said.

". . . Yeah, uh huh, early this morning, too," Mama said. "Said she was gone pay Tommy Lee for helpin'. I said it was all right."

"Well, what she want, Lue?"

"Would you believe—to tote that big 'ole welcome mat of hers. You 'member?"

Mabel shook her wig.

Mama gave her a look. "Mabel—the one she stitched up just after her mama and daddy passed . . ."

"Oh . . . yeah . . ."

"Had my baby tote that big 'ole thang to the dump."

"Uh uh, no she didn't."

"Yes, she did! I thought it was somethin' important—and on a Sunday, too."

"Um hum . . . on a Sunday."

"Course she paid him ten dollars. I told him that money should go in the collection plate, 'cause ain't nobody should be workin' on the Lord's Day. He gave me five of it."

Mabel nodded. "Yep, that's what I woulda done too, Lue. Um hum."

Mama Lucille rolled her eyes. "But that chile, Mabel, I swear she—"

Suddenly the choir stopped singing. Vanessa stopped playing the piano. Mabel and Mama Lucille stopped gossiping. The children stopped playing and giggling in the back. There was a hushed silence in the church. You'd have thought an angel of the Lord was making a visit. All heads faced the door. Luther looked up, too. His heart did somersaults. There stood Alura in the prettiest yellow dress. She was carrying the Bible Luther gave her for Christmas. She stood there unconsciously tugging at her dress. It was a might tight. She glanced around the room. There were a few whispers.

Alura was surprised to see Luther sitting in the pulpit. "Good morning," she said to Reverend Hayes and Reverend Eddings. "Somebody told me visitors were always welcomed." She looked up at Luther.

Reverend Hayes kept staring at her with his mouth open, trying to hold up his specs.

"Sorry I'm late," Alura apologized to the faces staring at her.

I felt Olivia start to get up to go get her, but I intentionally held her down. I slightly shook my head. Luther came down from the pulpit. He took her arm in his and walked her down the aisle to the seat next to Olivia. Alura's green eyes were a twinkling twin set of little ponds as she held onto Luther's arm for dear life.

Then Reverend Eddings cleared his throat and motioned for Vanessa to continue playing. Reverend Hayes finally found his vocal chords. "Yes . . . yes, welcome, Miss Simmons. We're very pleased you joined us this morning. Very pleased indeed."

After services, Olivia was giving Alura a hug. Mama and Mabel came over.

"Mornin', Miss Simmons," Mama said. "You look awful dooded up this mornin'. Look like you should be going some place else besides church."

Luther came over and put his hand inside Alura's. She squeezed his hand. "Why, thank you, Mother Williams, but haven't you heard? It's not where you're going that counts . . ." She looked up at Luther and her voice grew real soft. "It's who you are when you get there."

Luther preached his first sermon two weeks later called "Backing Off The Backbiting." After that day, Mabel and Mama Lucille never talked about nobody else in church. Mama said it was because Luther was a "man of the cloth," and since Alura was gonna be his wife, she wasn't about to make God mad at her. I love my mama and Aunt Mabel, God rest their souls. Mabel passed away first. She never got to see Alura finally "marry up with a good God-fearing man."

1993

LOS ANGELES

Chapter Fifteen

Young Jake, the outcome of Luther and Alura's marriage, ran through the emergency room. Nurses and visitors alike did a double-take as the tall, light-skinned, handsome young man in a gray Armani suit, briefcase in hand, charged up to the reception desk.

"I'm here to see Luther Rawlings," he said quickly.

The nurse stared at him. He had short curly red and brown hair. His emerald green shirt with matching tie, sparkled with his green eyes. "Are you a relative," she asked.

"I'm his son," he said, impatiently. "What room is he in?"

"Oh, just a minute." She was busy checking the roster.

Jake rubbed his hands together as he waited.

"He's in OR—"

Olivia came over to him and he hugged her. "You poor baby" Olivia told him. "I'll take you to the waiting room. Where's Hawk?"

"Uncle Hawk's parking the car." Jake hugged her and kissed her on her cheek. Then he sought Olivia's eyes for a clue. "How is he—really?"

Olivia shook her head. "There's no word yet. He got beat up bad. But don't worry, baby, Dr. Freeman is one of the best surgeons we have. It'll be all right."

Olivia took him to the waiting room. "I'll send in one of the volunteers in a minute, okay? I have to get back to my desk."

Young Jake nodded.

"Oh, and tell Hawk to page me when you hear anything. Anything at all, you hear?"

Jake nodded again and sunk down into one of the chairs. There were only four other people in the small waiting area. There was an elderly white woman who was falling asleep, a young white man and his daughter, and a young black woman. The black woman smiled at Jake. She started to speak to him, but decided against it.

Jake leaned forward and listened to Bill Cosby on the television monitor advertising Kodak film. "Capture the moment," Cosby was saying. A lot of moments ran through young Jake's mind. He remembered the time when he was eight years old and the teacher told them to write about what they wanted to be when they grew up.

Luther had picked him up from school. He was a bright child but the teacher said he talked too much. That day, Jake was quiet.

"You all right, Jake?" Luther asked.

His son nodded. He acted more mature than his age. "I need to talk about something, Daddy."

"Okay, shoot."

"I got something to show you," he said, reaching in his jeans and pulling out a folded piece of paper. "Promise you won't get mad."

"I promise."

Jake looked at him. "Swear on a ton of pitchers' mounts?"

Luther smiled. "Yeah, I swear."

"The teacher asked us to write about what we want to be when we grow up. And, Daddy, if it's all the same to you, I don't want to be a barber." He blinked his green eyes at Luther.

"All right. So what do you want to be?"

Jake's grin stretched across his small face. "A lawyer!"

Luther nodded and smiled.

"But Junior Stewart said he wants to be an astronaut, and that me being a lawyer is real stupid." Jake looked up at Luther. "It's not stupid is it, Daddy?"

Luther ruffled his son's curly head. "Nope, son, it's not. You have a right to be anything you want to be, because there's nobody who's gonna wear your shoes the way you do. You remember that."

Young Jake smiled and sat back in his seat. "I'll remember, Daddy."

Jake was obviously startled by my elderly, overweight body coming into the waiting area. My eyes and hands were full of questions.

"Nothing yet, Hawk" young Jake told me.

I sighed and sat next to him. The man in the corner nodded. I gave him a brief nod.

I thought about how I'd been sitting with Olivia and Luther in the waiting room at Florence Hospital four years ago. We couldn't understand how it happened so quickly. Alura was diagnosed with breast cancer six years ago, and two years after that Luther buried her next to his mama and Amanda.

The tumor had grown to the size of an orange. Alura never complained to Luther, even though he was sure something had to be wrong. Me and Olivia lived almost four hundred miles away in Los Angeles. Olivia was working part-time at a major Los Angeles hospital, and I owned Hawk's Hondas. I had retired and Tommy Lee was in charge, but I still enjoyed trying to sell a car every now and then. We had flown back to Coolidge to attend the funeral. Alura and Olivia had corresponded, so she was aware of what was happening. The doctor had informed Alura that the tumor was inoperable. Alura begged Olivia not to tell Luther, because she didn't want him to worry.

At Alura's funeral four years ago Luther shared both "good news and not-so-good news" with me. His son Jake had been accepted into law school with a full scholarship. That was, of course, the good news. Luther and young Jake had driven me and

Olivia back to the airport. Olivia asked Jake to go with her to check the baggage while Luther talked to me about old times. That's when Luther broke the "not-so-good news." At the time, I refused to believe it. I wasn't ready to lose my best friend.

"Doc says I have colon cancer," Luther had said matter-of-factly. "He's given me six months to a year—if I'm lucky, he said."

I knew Luther didn't believe in luck, but it must've been a miracle for him to still be alive now, four years later. I was quiet. Never said a word as Luther talked. I couldn't.

"I told the doc luck has nothing to do with it." Luther had sighed. "You know, Hawk, the way I look at it—it's . . . it's like being at the bottom of the ninth with two outs. And you and I both know from experience that just about anything can happen between that time."

I remember nodding and put my head down.

"Course, we all know the game's got to end some time. Now, I don't want to bother my boy Jake with this. He's got his studies to think about. And, God willing, I might get to see him graduate." Luther put his hand on my shoulder. "But if I don't, Hawk, I want you to make me a promise."

I bit my lip and took a deep breath. I nodded.

"In the envelope inside my will is a key to a box with that specially-autographed baseball that old Jake gave me . . . remember when we went to hear them read his will up in Phoenix?"

I nodded. Seemed all I could do.

"It's worth a lot. Probably get a few grand for it at any auction. That's my Jake's graduation present. All right?"

I had agreed, but my hope was that Luther would be there, when the time came, to give it to Jake himself. Now, if cancer wasn't bad enough, these young, racist, roughnecks had attacked him at the bus station. If only I was just ten years younger . . .

A girl dressed in a yellow smock came up to us. "Can I get you two anything?" she asked me and young Jake. "Some coffee? Tea? Water?"

Before I could tell her "no," the doctor came into the waiting area. Jake held his breath as he got to his feet. The doctor looked at both of us and decided Jake must be Luther's son.

"Mr. Jake Rawlings?" the doctor asked, reaching for Jake's hand.

Jake nodded, shaking his hand.

"He wants to see you," the doctor said. I watched Jake leave, and then turned to me. "Do you know a Mr. Hawk Williams?"

"Yeah—all my life."

The doctor nodded. "Apparently he's Mr. Rawlings' brother. Can you get a hold of him?"

I smiled in spite of myself. "You're talking to him." Like I said before, the way I figured it, Luther and me *were* brothers— brothers in the Lord, that is.

The doctor took a breath. "Oh. Very well. Mr. Rawlings said I should talk to you . . . You are aware of—"

"Yes. I am."

In the hospital room, young Jake took his father's hand. "I'll kill every one of them who did this to you," he promised.

Luther shook his head and tried to smile. His voice was weak. "No, I didn't . . . I didn't come out here . . . just to see *you* go to jail for the rest of your life . . . How about making sure . . . making sure they go to jail for a long . . . long time."

Jake promised his father he would. Silently, he promised himself he would become a prosecuting attorney. That was his goal.

The day of Jake's graduation, Olivia was sitting with me, watching proudly as young Jake walked across the stage in his blue and black robe to receive his diploma and give his valedictorian speech. Jake gripped the diploma with all his being. Then he leaned toward the mike, expertly balancing his cap. It was a wonderful speech, surely the best that me and Olivia ever heard. I could tell Jake had been listening intently to his father's sermons. I even heard him directly quote Luther a few times. Then Jake gave his honors.

"This diploma means more to me than most of you know. As for me, it will open up doors over and above that which I have imagined possible. I thank God for this opportunity. I've found that with his help, nothing is impossible. I thank my Aunt Olivia and Uncle Hawk. They have patiently and generously supported me, encouraged me, and, of course, been good friends these past few years. For that I'm truly grateful"

Jake stared down at his paper for a moment. He seemed to have no more words to read but so many words in his heart. "To my mother, who did not live to see this day, but who encouraged me and loved me through everything I've ever wanted to do. I miss her greatly, but a part of her is always with me."

Jake glanced up for a moment at the red light just over the heads of the crowd in the auditorium. "And, to my father . . . my dad—what can I tell you about someone like him? He's my best friend. My father happens to be a white man. Unfortunately, he was the victim of a racially-motivated assault a few days ago. I intend to make sure that the perpetrators don't go unpunished. I understand the anger, but somewhere down the line it all has to stop. I just want those young men to know that my father, Reverend Luther Rawlings, never judged people by the color of their skin. He loved everyone—in spite of themselves. And, he even prayed for all of you, and asked me to do the same."

Jake steadied himself on the podium. "Many of you are probably unaware that in 1967 there was one white man inducted not only into the National Athletes Hall of Fame but also into the Black Athletes Hall of Fame. That man's name is Branch Rickey. Why is he, a white man, in the Black Athletes Hall of Fame, you might ask? Very simple. Because in his infinite wisdom, he signed Jackie Robinson in 1946. And in 1947 Jackie Robinson became the first black man to play ball in the major leagues—opening up the way for all other black baseball players." Jake's voice cracked. "You see,

I feel like Jackie right now, and my father, Reverend Luther Rawlings, is—and always will be—*my* Branch Rickey. I love you, Dad. Thank you all very much and God bless you."

Jake received a standing ovation. Olivia stood with me as we proudly applauded him in the auditorium. He had another fan in a hospital room in Los Angeles applauding him also. Luther's eyes were full of paternal pride and tears as he admired his son's handsome face beaming into his room by satellite. Luther would never have dreamed they could do such a thing. The nurse sniffed and heaved a delighted sigh as Luther, clad in his hospital gown, sat up, wiping tears from his eyes. His body ached, and he knew it was time for his medication, but he didn't care. He was glad to be able to feel pain—to be able to feel anything. And maybe Doc Freeman could work a miracle.

His aging eyes had a dim glimmer. The twitching had finally stopped. He knew he'd be getting a big hug from his son, as well as from me and Olivia in about an hour. He nodded and smiled at the nurse with as much strength as he could muster. "That's my son," Luther said in a satisfied and determined voice. He knew visiting hours would be over soon, but he didn't care. "*That* is *my* son," he repeated again.

The nurse got up to leave, and switched off the light as Luther leaned back against the soft cushiony pillow Alura had made for him many years ago. He closed his eyes. He thought he saw Alura, Amanda, his mama and old Jake.

"Boy, you done good," he heard old Jake whisper to him before he went to sleep.